Music by

Benny
Anderrson

Björn
Ulvaeus

Lyrics

Tim
Rice

Based on an Idea by
Tim Rice

Book by
Richard Nelson

A SAMUEL FRENCH ACTING EDITION

SAMUEL FRENCH

FOUNDED 1830

NEW YORK HOLLYWOOD LONDON TORONTO

SAMUELFRENCH.COM

ISBN 978-0-573-68917-8   Printed in U.S.A.   #5236

Chess premiered in London at the Prince Edward Theatre on May 14, 1986. It was presented by Three Knights Ltd., the Shubert Organization and Robert Fox Ltd. for Chess Productions Ltd with the following soloists (in order of vocal appearance):

Mayor of Merano	Richard Mitchell
Frederick Trumper	Murray Head
Florence Vassy	Elaine Paige
Alexander Molokov	John Turner
Anatoly Sergievsky	Tommy Korberg
Walter de Courcey	Kevin Colson
The Arbiter	Tom Jobe
Principal TV Presenter	Peter Karrie
Civil Servants	Richard Lyndon and Paul Wilson
Svetlana Sergievsky	Siobhan McCarthy

THE COMPANY (in alphabetic order):
Leo Andrew, Julie Armstrong, Yvonne Bachem, Julia Birch, Richard Courtice, Catherine Coffee, Annie Cox, Hugh Craig, Geoffrey Dallamore, Carol Duffy, Garrick Forbes, Wayne Fowkes, Aliki Georgiou, Philip Griffith, Peter Karrie, Donna King, Madeline Loftin, Patrick Long, Kim Lonsdale, Richard Lyndon, Richard Mitchell, Gail Mortley, Kerri Murphy, Mhairi Nelson, Anita Pashley, William Pool, Jane Powell, Grainne Rennihan, Richard Sampson, Jacqui Scott, DuncanSmith, Sandy Strallen, Suzanne Thomas, Sally Ann Triplett, Oke Wambu, Hilary Western, Paul Wilson

Chess was presented by the Shubert Organization on April 28, 1988 at the Imperial Theatre. It was directed by Trevor Nunn with dance staging by Lynne Taylor-Corbett; scenic design by Robin Wagner; costume design by Theoni V. Aldredge; lighting design by David Hersey and sound design by Andrew Bruce. The cast was as follows:

GREGOR VASSY	Neal Ben-Ari
Young FLORENCE	Gina Gallagher
FREDDIE	Philip Casnoff
FLORENCE	Judy Kuhn
ANATOLY	David Carroll
MOLOKOV	Harry Goz
NICKOLAI	Kurt Johns
WALTER	Dennis Parlato
ARBITER	Paul Harman
SVETLANA	Marcia Mitzman
JOE and HAROLD	Richard Muenz and Eric Johnson

Ensemble: John Aller, Neal Ben-Ari, Suzanne Briar, Steve Clemente, Katherine Lynee Condit, Ann Crumb, David Cryer, R.F. Daley, Deborah Beneviere, Kurt Johns, Eric Johnson, Paul Laureano, Rosemary Loar, Judy McLane, Jessica Molaskey, Richard Muenz, Kip Niven, Francis Ruivivar, Alex Santoriello, Wysandria Woolsey
Swings: Karen Babcock, Craig Wells

Note: Vocal selections available for $12.95 plus postage.

CHARACTERS

FLORENCE
FREDDIE
ANATOLY
MOLOKOV
SVETLANA
WALTER
ARBITER
GREGORY VASSY
YOUNG FLORENCE
NIKOLAI
JOE
HAROLD
ENSEMBLE

CHARACTER BREAKDOWN

Florence: Strong belt voice (to E). Mid-thirties. Born in Hungary (so musn't look like an "All-American Girl"); has been brought up in America since 1956. She is clever, theatrical, touching, vivacious, volatile. Frederick's chess "second."

Freddie: Rock tenor (to C). Mid-thirties. An American chess champion. A cross between Bobby Fisher and John McEnroe. Arrogant and temperamental, but a genius; his chess playing is revolutionary. We need to see his artistry along with his danger and his obsessiveness.

Anatoly: Baritone (to G sharp). Early forties. A Russian chess champion. Unexpectedly charming. He doesn't seem a romantic hero at first, but becomes one through his personality. An intelligent, feeling, passionate man.

Molokov: Bass (down to F sharp). Fifties. *Not* a fake, comic, stage Russian. Intellectually formidable. Seemingly a father figure to Florence. Anatoly's chess "second." An actor who sings well.

Svetlana: Strong belt voice. Late thirties. Anatoly's wife. Domestic, wholesome, homey. A dramatic contrast to Florence—*not* a contemporary cosmopolitan woman.

Walter: Bass-baritone (down to G sharp). Fifties. A marketing agent. Seemingly respectable, substantial, trustworthy. An actor who sings well.

Arbiter: Rock high baritone (up to A). Thirty to early forties. International businessman. Smooth, but with a quick temper.

MUSICAL NUMBERS
ACT I

PROLOGUE .... BUDAPEST, HUNGARY, 1956
The Story of Chess .... Gregor

BANGKOK, THAILAND, THE PRESENT TIME

Freddie's Entrance .... Freddie
Press Conference .... Freddie, Florence, Reporters
Where I Want to be .... Anatoly
Argument .... Florence, Freddie
Merchandisers .... Walter, Merchandisers
Diplomats .... Molokov, American &
Soviet Delegates
Quartet .... Molokov, Florence,
Arbiter, Anatoly
Florence/American .... Florence, Freddie
Someone Else's Story .... Florence
One Night in Bangkok .... Freddie and Company
Terrace Duet .... Florence, Anatoly
Florence Quits .... Freddie, Florence
A Taste of Pity .... Freddie
Nobody's Side .... Florence
Reporters .... Reporters
Anthem .... Anatoly

INTERMISSION
ACT II

Prologue (Optional) .... KENNEDY AIRPORT, NY, 8 WEEKS LATER
Arbiter's Song .... Arbiter and Company

BUDAPEST, HUNGARY

Hungarian Folk Song .... Company
Heaven Help My Heart .... Florence
Winning .... Freddie, Walter
You and I .... Anatoly, Florence, Svetlana
Freddie Goes Metal .... Freddie
Let's Work Together .... Walter, Molokov
I Know Him So Well .... Florence, Svetlana
Pity the Child .... Freddie
Father's Lullaby (Apukah Eros Kezen) .... Gregor, Florence
Endgame .... Anatoly, Freddie & Company
You and I (reprise) .... Anatoly, Florence
Finale (reprise) .... Florence

CHESS

[MUSIC #1: PROLOGUE]

Budapest, Hungary, 1956. A small crowded room; numerous people under blankets sleeping, others smoking, reading the paper or simply staring into space; all are waiting.

In the center of this, GREGOR VASSY, mid-thirties, sits in front of a chess board; his four-year-old daughter, FLORENCE, sits across from him. Outside one hears the occasional GUNSHOT.

TWO MEN and a WOMEN, all with guns, enter. FLORENCE turns to them.

GREGOR. Florence, please concentrate.

[THE STORY OF CHESS]

GREGOR. (*Singing.*)
EACH GAME OF CHESS MEANS THERE'S ONE LESS
VARIATION LEFT TO BE PLAYED
EACH DAY GOT THROUGH MEANS ONE OR TWO
LESS MISTAKES REMAIN TO BE MADE

NOT MUCH IS KNOWN
OF EARLY DAYS OF CHESS BEYOND A FAIRLY VAGUE REPORT
THAT FIFTEEN HUNDRED YEARS AGO TWO PRINCES FOUGHT,
THOUGH BROTHERS, FOR A HINDU THRONE

THEIR MOTHER CRIED
FOR NO-ONE REALLY LIKES THEIR OFFSPRING FIGHTING TO THE DEATH

SHE BEGGED THEM STOP THE SLAUGHTER
   WITH HER EVERY BREATH
BUT SURE ENOUGH ONE BROTHER DIED

SAD BEYOND BELIEF
SHE TOLD HER WINNING SON
"YOU HAVE CAUSED SUCH GRIEF—
I CAN'T BELIEVE THIS EVIL THING YOU'VE
   DONE"

HE TRIED TO EXPLAIN
HOW THINGS HAD REALLY BEEN
BUT HE TRIED IN VAIN
NO WORDS OF HIS COULD SATISFY THE QUEEN

AND SO HE ASKED THE WISEST MEN HE KNEW
THE WAY TO LESSEN HER DISTRESS
THEY TOLD HIM HE'D BE PRETTY CERTAIN TO
   IMPRESS
BY USING MODEL SOLDIERS ON
A CHECQUERED BOARD TO SHOW IT WAS HIS
   BROTHER'S FAULT ...
THEY THUS INVENTED CHESS

(Some PEOPLE hurry in.)

   MAN. The archway's clear.
   WOMAN. The Russians have moved into Prodgsy
Street.
   A MAN IN THE ROOM. Let's go. Hurry!

(Most of the PEOPLE in the room pick up their
belongings and start to go.)

   GREGOR. Go with them, Florence. Please go! *(He*
tries to hand her to a woman.)
   YOUNG FLORENCE. Papa—
   GREGOR. Go!

(She is carried out with the group. A few remain.)

MAN IN ROOM. Good luck, Gregor Vassy.
MAN FROM FIRST GROUP. Ferenc says that if they move across the river, we move back to the wall.
ANOTHER MAN WHO ENTERED. And if they stay at the wall?
FIRST MAN WHO ENTERED. We move to the Margaret Bridge.
GREGOR. We move, they move.
(Sings.)
EACH GAME OF CHESS MEANS THERE ONE LESS VARIATION LEFT TO BE …
(Spoken.) Let's go.

(He picks up a gun and they follow him out. EXPLOSION.)

End of Prologue

ACT I

Scene 1

Bangkok today. A large meeting room in the Bangkok Hilton Hotel. A large banner behind reads: THE HILTON WELCOMES THE WORLD CHESS CHAMPIONSHIP. As the scene begins FREDDIE is coming down the hallway, followed by a crowd, including FLORENCE.

[MUSIC #2: FREDDIE'S ENTRANCE]

FREDDIE. *(Singing.)*
WHAT A SCENE! WHAT A JOY!

WHAT A LOVELY SIGHT
WHEN MY GAME IS THE BIG SENSATION
HAS THE MOB'S SPORTING TASTE
ALTERED OVERNIGHT?
HAVE YOU FOUND NEW SOPHISTICATION?

NOT YET! YOU JUST WANT TO SEE
IF THE NICE GUY (*He points to ANATOLY.*) BEATS
　　THE BUM (*He indicates himself.*)
IF IT'S EAST-WEST
AND THE MONEY'S SKY-HIGH
YOU ALL COME, YOU ALL COME

*(As they enter the meeting room there is pandemonium.
　　Also at the table are ANATOLY and MOLOKOV.)*

PRESS REPRESENTATIVE. Questions for Mr.
Anatoly Sergievsky, the World Chess champion, and
Freddie Trumper, the challenger.
　　REPORTERS. Freddie!!!!
　　FREDDIE. You!
　　FRENCH REPORTER. (*In French.*) Mr. Trumper,
What is you—?
　　FREDDIE. I don't speak Frog, next question!
　　AUSTRALIAN REPORTER. Mr. Trumper, do
you think chess should be an Olympic sport?
　　FREDDIE. What, and do it for free?!
　　AMERICAN REPORTER. What are your
impressions of Bangkok so far, Freddie?
　　FREDDIE. Geez—I'm staying right here at the
Hilton. I'm driving an Olds Cutlass. Right down the
block's not only a McDonald's but a Burger King. Seems
like Cleveland to me.

(Laughter.)

ENGLISH REPORTER. In Budapest you're scheduled at the same time as the next summit conference between—

FREDDIE. If we make it to Budapest. Hey, I could win them all here. He could just give up.

ENGLISH REPORTER. Yes, but do you think these series of summits have now depoliticized contests like these?

FREDDIE. If they had would creeps like you be here?

ANOTHER REPORTER. Freddie—?

FREDDIE. My advice to the President of the United States is—The only time you believe an utterance from a Russian is when he cuts the cheese.

PRESS REPRESENTATIVE. Now some questions for Mr. Sergievsky.

GERMAN REPORTER. Mr. Sergievsky, this is only the second time that a match has been divided between two sites, Bangkok and Budapest in this case. This arrangement suggests to me that you, as the world champion, have found it necessary to compromise—

MOLOKOV. I shall speak to that. (*FREDDIE pretends to snore and sleep.*) Mr. Sergievsky plays where the World Chess Federation tells him to play. The match sites are not under our control.

AMERICAN REPORTER. Freddie—?

FREDDIE. (*Pretending to wake up.*) What?! Is somebody talking to me? (*Laughter from the reporters.*)

AMERICAN REPORTER. Bangkok's got a reputation for having a rather rich nightlife. (*Some laughter.*) Are you planning to partake while—?

FREDDIE. I'm in training. I'm sorry to say. Next time.

ANOTHER REPORTER. You probably brought all you need with you, anyway. (*Laughter.*)

FREDDIE. (*Smiling.*) What's that supposed to mean?

REPORTER. Miss Vassy's not an unattractive woman, Freddie.

FREDDIE. Florence is my second. What are you implying?

REPORTER. Forget it.

FREDDIE. No, I want to know—

FLORENCE. (*Trying to stop this.*) Freddie—

FREDDIE. (*He shakes her off. To reporter.*) Come here. (*Awkward pause.*) Come here.

REPORTER. (*As he approaches FREDDIE.*) Look, it was a joke. Okay?

(*Suddenly FREDDIE picks up a glass of water and throws it in the Reporter's face.*)

[MUSIC #2A: PRESS CONFERENCE]

(*FREDDIE hurries out. There is chaos; REPORTERS yelling questions.*)

[SMILE YOU GOT YOUR FIRST
EXCLUSIVE STORY]

FIRST REPORTER. (*Singing.*)
WELL, WHAT DID I SAY?
HE'S OUT OF HIS TREE
SECOND REPORTER.
HE'S FINALLY FLIPPED
AND BETWEEN YOU AND ME
THIRD REPORTER.
THOUGH HE SWEARS THE AMERICAN DREAM
IS CLEARLY THE BEST
HE'S NO ADVERTISEMENT FOR
LIFE AND TIME IN THE WEST.
FLORENCE.
SMILE YOU GOT YOUR FIRST EXCLUSIVE STORY
NOW YOU CAN BASK IN HIS REFLECTED GLORY
"NAKED, UNPROVOKED, YANKEE AGGRESSION"

OH, WHAT A CREDIT TO YOUR GREAT
PROFESSION!
REPORTERS.
HOW SAD THAT THE BEST HIS COUNTRY'S
PRODUCED
IS CRUMBLING IN FRONT OF OUR EYES AND
REDUCED
TO A MINDLESS ABUSE,
WHEN HE SHOULD BE GRATEFUL INSTEAD
REMEMBER WE MADE HIM FAMOUS
WITHOUT US HE'S DEAD.

TELL ALL THIS TO THE UNITED NATIONS
IS HE AN ASSET TO EAST-WEST RELATIONS?

End of Scene

ACT I

Scene 2

Hotel hallway and later. Anatoly's hotel suite.
ANATOLY and MOLOKOV are on their way down the
hall.

ANATOLY. It's all a performance. It has to be.
MOLOKOV. Even I knew his reputation.
ANATOLY. But to see it there in front of you.
MOLOKOV. Yes, very amusing.

(A RUSSIAN approaches them from behind.)

RUSSIAN. Molokov, you have telephone messages.
(Hands them to him. To ANATOLY.) Good luck,
Sergievsky. *(Back to MOLOKOV.)* The American's just
a child.

MOLOKOV. I'm beginning to think a chess match will not be the boring assignment I had feared. (*As they enter the suite, hands ANATOLY a phone message.*) From your wife. She called from home.

ANATOLY. You'll learn that when I'm in a match I have neither a wife nor a ...

MOLOKOV. A home? (*Beat. Continues to look through messages.*) When you *are* home I understand you don't call your wife either. But this is none of my business.

ANATOLY. I'm here to play chess.

MOLOKOV. And I'm here to help you play chess. (*Turns to NIKOLAI.*) What did you bring?

NIKOLAI. (*Handing file.*) The woman with Trumper. Florence Vassy.

ANATOLY. (*He has sat at a table where a chess board is set up; without looking up.*) An experienced second. She's well-known. You could have just asked me.

MOLOKOV. (*Reading the file.*) Hungarian refugee. Left Budapest as a child. 1956. (*To NIKOLAI.*) Sleep together?

NIKOLAI. Rumor is they don't anymore. She has her own room here. But we're checking this out ourselves.

ANATOLY. (*Over chess board.*) He needs only an answer, Nikolai, not a videotape.

MOLOKOV. Speak for yourself! (*He laughs. ANATOLY doesn't. MOLOKOV nods and NIKOLAI goes.*) Hungarian women. I had a crush on one in Moscow. But just because I was Russian ...

ANATOLY. The sacrifices we Russian men have had to make for the cause of world peace.

(*PHONE rings. MOLOKOV picks it up.*)

MOLOKOV. Hello? I'll be right down. (*Hangs up. As he goes to door.*) Our ambassador has arrived.

FLORENCE. I suggest the head, something you don't seem to use anymore.

FREDDIE. Get off me.

FLORENCE. Watch him. That is my advice. Period.

FREDDIE. I know what I'm doing.

FLORENCE. That I am going to have to take on faith.

FREDDIE. Sergievsky doesn't know what the hell to make of me after this morning.

FLORENCE. Stick to the chess, Freddie. Do what you are good at. (*Beat.*) The Russians aren't as dumb as you think. Sergievsky may not have just sold his toes for twenty-five grand, but we can still have some respect for him.

(*He looks at her, starts to say something in his defense, stops and looks back at the board. Short pause.*)

FLORENCE. (*Without looking up.*) And from now on this agent or whatever he is stays away from you while you're preparing.

FREDDIE. What are you, my mother? You're not here to tell me what to do, Florence.

FLORENCE. I thought that's exactly what my job was, Freddie. (*They look at each other. Suddenly she looks back at the board.*) Here, a pawn down. (*She takes off a pawn.*) The bishop … I move the knight …

(*He moves. She moves. He moves. She moves.*)

FREDDIE. (*Smiles, realizes defeat.*) Okay. Very good. Where'd you pick that up—?

FLORENCE. Belinski in Philadelphia. He saw this position in a Sergievsky match in Volograd. (*Beat.*) I've been saving it.

FREDDIE. (*Conceding.*) So—I won't let myself get into a position like—

ANATOLY. Our ambassador?

[MUSIC #3: WHERE I WANT TO BE]

MOLOKOV. Didn't I tell you? He's asked to play a single game against the world's Champion.

ANATOLY. Tonight? No, Molokov—

MOLOKOV. (*At the door.*) He went to university with the First Secretary. (*Beat.*) You have no choice. (*He exits. Pause.*)

(*ANATOLY looks over the chess board.*)

ANATOLY. (*Singing.*)
WHO NEEDS A DREAM?
WHO NEEDS AMBITION?
WHO'D BE THE FOOL
IN MY POSITION?
ONCE I HAD DREAMS
NOW THEY'RE OBSESSIONS
HOPES BECAME NEEDS
LOVERS POSSESSIONS

THEN THEY MOVE IN
OH SO DISCREETLY
SLOWLY AT FIRST
SMILINGLY TOO SWEETLY
I OPENED DOORS
THEY WALKED RIGHT THROUGH THEM
CALLED ME THEIR FRIEND
I HARDLY KNEW THEM.

NOW I'M WHERE I WANT TO BE AND WHO I
    WANT TO BE AND DOING WHAT I ALWAYS
    SAID I WOULD AND YET I FEEL I HAVEN'T
    WON AT ALL
RUNNING FOR MY LIFE AND NEVER LOOKING
    BACK

IN CASE THERE'S SOMEONE RIGHT BEHIND TO
   SHOOT ME DOWN AND SAY HE ALWAYS
   KNEW I'D FALL

WHEN THE CRAZY WHEEL SLOWS DOWN
WHERE WILL I BE? BACK WHERE I STARTED

DON'T GET ME WRONG
I'M NOT COMPLAINING
TIMES HAVE BEEN GOOD
FAST, ENTERTAINING
BUT WHAT'S THE POINT
IF I'M CONCEALING
MOST OF MY THOUGHTS
ALL OF MY FEELING

NOW I'M WHERE I WANT TO BE AND WHO I
   WANT
TO BE AND DOING WHAT I ALWAYS SAID I
   WOULD
AND YET I FEEL I HAVEN'T WON AT ALL
RUNNING FOR MY LIFE AND NEVER LOOKING
   BACK
IN CASE THERE'S SOMEONE RIGHT BEHIND
TO SHOOT ME DOWN AND SAY HE ALWAYS
   KNEW
I'D FALL

WHEN THE CRAZY WHEEL SLOWS DOWN
WHERE WILL I BE? BACK WHERE I STARTED.

End of Scene

[MUSIC #3A: WHERE I WANT TO BE—PLAYOFF]

ACT I

Scene 3

*Freddie's suite. FREDDIE and FLORENCE are playi
chess/practicing. WALTER is on the phone.*

WALTER. (*Into phone.*) Thirty thousand. He won
take a penny less. (*Calls.*) Will you, Freddie? (*FREDDI.*
doesn't respond; into phone.) He's adamant. It's thirty o
nothing. (*Beat.*) No, thirty. (*Beat.*) It's a deal. Twenty-
five. Lou, see you at my little show I hope. (*Hangs up.*)
Twenty-five grand and it doesn't even have to be your
foot in the picture.
FREDDIE. It doesn't? (*Makes a chess move.*)
WALTER. They can use any foot they want. They
put your signature across it, see. (*Beat.*) One ad. They
don't even need to photograph you. They can pull
something.

(*FREDDIE looks up.*)

FLORENCE. Freddie, please. Concentrate.
WALTER. (*Takes out a pack of cigarettes. It i
empty, he crushes it and gets up.*) A photo session, I tol
them, was going to cost real money. Excuse me, I'
already late. The trade show's just beginning. Florence
if you feel like slumming. (*WALTER leaves.*)
FLORENCE. (*Mimicking.*) "A photo session v
going to cost real money." Where did you find that g
selling watches on Broadway?
FREDDIE. You just hate the idea of making mo
don't you?
FLORENCE. I hate the fact of always talking ;
it. Now that he's sold your feet, what other parts of
body are you going to throw in?
FREDDIE. Florence—

FLORENCE. (*She grabs his hand.*) Sergievsky wasn't the one who made the move, Frederick. He was the one who got out of it.

FREDDIE. (*Is stunned.*) No, Florence. There's no— (*He gets up, then looks back at the board.*) No. That's not possible.

FLORENCE. Sergievsky found a way out.

FREDDIE. You must have it wrong. (*He goes into the bathroom*)

[MUSIC #4: ARGUMENT]

FLORENCE. He got out! (*Calling through the door.*) It's not going to be as easy as you think, Mr. Trumper!! (*Pause. She sits, sighs ...*)

[HOW MANY WOMEN]

FLORENCE. (*Sings.*)
HOW MANY WOMEN WOULD DRIVE THEM-
SELVES CRAZY
BY ARGUING OVER A GAME OF CHESS?
NOT VERY MANY—THE WAY THINGS ARE
GOING
THERE'LL SOON BE ONE LESS!
FREDDIE. (*Shouting from shower.*)
DON'T BELIEVE YOU SWEETIE PIE—
FLORENCE.
LISTEN—I HAD AMBITIONS
HOW DID I GET WAYLAID?
HOW CAN SUCH A FLOWER,
A SENSITIVE SOUL, A DELICATE CHILD
WIND UP AS NURSEMAID
RESPECTABLY SET FOR THE GLITTERING
PRIZES
INSTEAD OF WHICH I LANDED YOU—
FREDDIE. (*Enter.*)
YOU'LL GET YOUR PRIZES!

I'M NINETY PERCENT OF THE WAY TO THE TOP
   OF THE HEAP.
   FLORENCE.
THANKS — 10%—YOU GOT ME CHEAP
   FREDDIE. (*Speaking.*) No, no, Florence—I meant
we are ninety percent of the way—
   FLORENCE.
HOW MANY WOMEN—ARTICULATE WOMEN,
   WITH
SOMETHING TO SHOUT ABOUT—SPEND THEIR
   TIME
PLAYING A GAME IN WHICH SILENCE IS
   GOLDEN
AND SPEAKING A CRIME?
   FREDDIE.
MAYBE IF HE MOVED HIS KING...
   FLORENCE.
ALL OF MY STRUGGLES FOR QUALIFICATION—
   MY
NIGHTS WITH GOETHE AND PROUST
RECKLESSLY ABANDONED
FOR YOU! WHO THINKING CHEKHOV IS KING
   TO G3
AND JOYCE MY COLLEGE ROOMMATE!
BUT THEN WHEN I SHOW YOU A MOVE YOU
   CAN'T FATHOM
I HAVE TO ADMIT IT FEELS GREAT—
   FREDDIE.
GREAT NEWS FOR CHESS FANS! (*Making
   triumphant move.*)
YEAH—THAT'S HOW HE DID IT—YES, THAT'S
   HOW THE COMMUNIST PLAYS!
   FLORENCE.
MAYBE I DESERVE A RAISE.
   (*Speaking.*) Nice. (*Beat.*) Maybe you are ready for the
Russians.

End of Scene

ACT I

Scene 4

[MUSIC #5: MERCHANDISERS]

A large hall where a chess trade show is going on.

CHORUS.
WHEN YOU GET UP IN THE MORNING.
TILL YOU CRASH AT NIGHT
YOU WILL FIND YOURSELF SURROUNDED
BY OUR COPYRIGHT.

BRUSH YOUR TEETH WITH CHECKERED
 TOOTHPASTE
WEAR OUR VESTS
OUR KINGS AND QUEENS ON BOUNCING
 BREASTS
WALTER.
YOU COULD EVEN BUY A SET AND AND LEARN
 TO PLAY
CHORUS.
WE DON'T MIND—WE'LL SELL YOU SOMETHING
 ANYWAY.
—SELL YOU SOMETHING ANYWAY!!

MOLOKOV. Miss Vassy. Wonderful show, isn't it?

FLORENCE. Makes you feel—

MOLOKOV. Proud to be an American?

FLORENCE. What do you want, Mr. Molokov?

MOLOKOV. You've learned my name. I'm flattered.
(*Beat.*) A question about the chairs.

FLORENCE. We agreed on Swedish chairs. Neutral
chairs.

MOLOKOV. We brought with us two very com-
fortable Finnish chairs. (*Beat.*) Finland's neutral.

FLORENCE. But are the chairs?
MOLOKOV. You seem so distrustful. I hope you are not one of those right-wing conservative Americans—
FLORENCE. Not yet. But keep talking.

[MUSIC #6: DIPLOMATS]

(FLORENCE walks off. Molokov laughs. An AMERICAN approaches.)

1ST AMERICAN. What's funny, Mr. Molokov?
MOLOKOV. Miss Vassy—A humorous woman.

(Another AMERICAN approaches.)

2ND AMERICAN. What a pleasure to see opposing delegations getting along.

(A RUSSIAN has joined them)

FIRST RUSSIAN. The world is changing.
MOLOKOV. (*Sings.*)
NO ONE CAN DENY THESE ARE ENCOURAGING
    TIMES
    ALL.
NO ONE CAN DENY THESE ARE ENCOURAGING
    TIMES
    MOLOKOV.
IT'S THE U.S. VERSUS U.S.S.R.
YET WE MORE OR LESS ARE—
    ALL.
NO ONE CAN DENY THESE ARE ENCOURAGING
    TIMES
    MOLOKOV.
—TO OUR CREDIT PUTTING ALL THAT ASIDE
WE HAVE SWALLOWED OUR PRIDE

ALL.
THESE ARE OPTIMISTIC AND ENCOURAGING
  TIMES
2nd AMERICAN.
IT REALLY DOESN'T MATTER
WHO COMES OUT ON TOP
WHO GETS THE CHOP
  MOLOKOV.
NO-ONE'S WAY OF LIFE IS THREATENED BY A
  FLOP
  AMERICANS.
WHAT A LOAD OF WHINING PEASANTS!
THINKING THEY CAN WIN—THEY CAN'T
WHAT AN EXHIBITION OF SELF-DELUSION
THIS ONE'S A FOREGONE CONCLUSION
  MOLOKOV/RUSSIANS.
WE DON'T WANT THE WHOLE WORLD SAYING
THEY CAN'T EVEN WIN A GAME
WE HAVE NEVER RECKONED
ON COMING SECOND
THERE'S NO USE IN LOSING.
  MOLOKOV.
HOW GOOD TO FEEL THAT AS THIS GREAT
  EVENT BEGINS
IT UNDERPINS
OUR QUEST FOR PEACE, THE BONDS OF
  COMMON INTEREST
OF EAST AND WEST
  AMERICANS.
AS LONG AS OUR MAN WINS
  RUSSIANS.
AS LONG AS OUR MAN
  ALL.
  —WINS!!

[MUSIC #7 OPENING 1ST GAME]

ACT I

Scene 5

[MUSIC #7A: CHESS #1]

The Arena and later, elevators and Arbiter's office.
CHESS MUSIC (instrumental) begins. ANATOLY
and FREDDIE, at the chess board, begin to play. They
play for quite a while, when FREDDIE looks up at
ANATOLY, who is eating a cup of yogurt (he had
eaten another cup at the start of play). FREDDIE looks
at the yogurt, then back at ANATOLY.

FREDDIE. Put that down.
ANATOLY. (*In Russian.*) What? *Shtaw?*
FREDDIE. The yogurt. Give that here, let me see
that. (*He reaches across the board.*)
ANATOLY. (*In Russian.*) I'm not giving you my—
Nee dam— (*In English.*) Get away. (*He pulls the yogurt*
away.)
FREDDIE. (*Stands and yells.*) Check it! I want
someone checking that yogurt! (*To ANATOLY.*) Put it
down!

(Pause.
No one knows what to do. The ARBITER finally nods to
an assistant to go and look at the yogurt.)

ASSISTANT. (*As he goes to ANATOLY, then*
stops.) Check it for what?
FREDDIE. Check it!!
ANATOLY. (*Covering the yogurt, in English.*) This
is crazy? Why should I let you look at my yogurt?

(ASSISTANT is caught in the middle.)

FREDDIE. It's strawberry yogurt! I saw it was strawberry!

ANATOLY. This is true.

FREDDIE. (*Pleased.*) And before that it was blueberry!! (*Short pause.*)

ARBITER. So?

FREDDIE. What, are you stupid? He's getting signals. (*Beat.*) With the choice of yogurt. (*Beat.*) He's cheating!!!

ARBITER. Mr. Trumper …

FREDDIE. Don't be so damn naive!!

ANATOLY. (*In Russian, to MOLOKOV.*) Is this a joke? *EH-ta SHOOT-ka?*

FREDDIE. Do you see him showing us his yogurt? He is cheating. Just look at his face! (*Beat.*) I demand he no longer be served yogurt and I want an apology!

ANATOLY. (*In Russian.*) Never. (*Laughs.*) *Nee-za-SHTAW.*

FLORENCE. (*Approaching FREDDIE.*) Freddie, what are you—?

FREDDIE. (*To FLORENCE.*) I think I'm being very generous here. I could demand he be disqualified. (*Beat.*) Come on. (*Pause. To ARBITER.*) Call him on it! You are the arbiter. (*No response.*) Okay, I get it. You're working for him.

ARBITER. Mr. Trumper—Would you please—

FREDDIE. Forget it then! This match is history!! It's over!!

(*FREDDIE storms out. The CROWD gasps. Then silence.*)

ARBITER. (*Stands; beat:*) Break for lunch!

[MUSIC #8: quartet]

(*Chaos, REPORTERS run off after FREDDIE.*)

ANATOLY. (*To FLORENCE.*) Pity, you cannot always choose who you work for.

FLORENCE. True. (*Beat.*) And I've noticed you seem to have the same problem.

(The ARBITER leaves for the elevators and his office, followed by MOLOKOV, then FLORENCE and ANATOLY.)

MOLOKOV. (*To Arbiter.*)
WE WISH, NO MUST, MAKE OUR DISGUST
FOR THIS ABUSE PERFECTLY CLEAR
WE'RE HERE FOR CHESS—
ARE THE U.S.?
IF SO WHY FOUL THE ATMOSPHERE?
  FLORENCE.
I MUST PROTEST—OUR DELEGATION
HAS A HOST OF VALID POINTS TO RAISE
  ARBITER.
IT'S NOT JUST BLACK AND WHITE
IF I MAY COIN A PHRASE
AS ANY NEUTRAL WOULD ATTEST

(They pass into the hallway, in front of the elevators.)

  FLORENCE.
THOUGH WE CONCEDE (*She now sings to ANATOLY.*)
THE FACT YOUR MASTERS BEND THE RULES IS MAYBE NOT YOUR FAULT
IF THEY WITHDRAW THEIR PSYCHOLOGICAL ASSAULT
THEN UNDER PROTEST HE'LL PROCEED
  MOLOKOV.
IF YOUR MAN'S SO SWEET
THEN WHY HIS FIGHTING TALK?
IF HE SAYS WE CHEAT

THEN WHY ON EARTH DID HE GO TAKE A
WALK?
FLORENCE.
I AM NOT SURPRISED HE WANTED FRESHER AIR
ONCE HE REALIZED THERE WAS NO HOPE
OF YOUR GUYS PLAYING FAIR

FLORENCE &	**MOLOKOV &**
ANATOLY.	**ARBITER.**
HOW SAD	IT'S VERY SAD TO SEE
TO SEE	THE ANCIENT AND
	DISTINGUISHED GAME
	THAT USED TO BE

ALL.
A MODEL OF DECORUM AND TRANQUILITY
BECOME LIKE ANY OTHER SPORT
A BATTLEGROUND FOR RIVAL IDEOLOGIES
TO SLUG IT OUT WITH GLEE

*(They continue as the ARBITER and MOLOKOV get into
an elevator.)*

ANATOLY.
I WOULD SAY
WITH REGARD TO HIM
IT IS HARD TO REBUT
EVER-GROWING
SUSPICIONS
MY OPPOSITION'S A NUT
FLORENCE.
I WOULD HAVE SAID
YOU'D UNDERSTAND THE STRAIN AND
PRESSURE GETTING WHERE HE'S GOT
FOR THEN YOU'D SIMPLY CALL HIM HIGHLY-
STRUNG AND NOT
IMPLY THAT HE WAS OFF HIS HEAD
ANATOLY.
BUT HOW ON EARTH CAN SOMEONE EVEN
HALF AS CIVILIZED AND NICE AS YOU

BE PART OF SUCH A SELF-DESTRUCTIVE
POINT OF VIEW
I HOPE HE PAYS YOU
WHAT YOU'RE WORTH

(ANATOLY and FLORENCE get into second elevator.
ARBITER and MOLOKOV are seen in their elevator.)

   ARBITER.
I CALL THIS TUNE
NO ONE'S IMMUNE
TO MY POWER
ONCE IN THAT HALL
   MOLOKOV.
IN THAT CASE
I MUST ASK YOU
WHY YOU NOW
PRESIDE OVER A BRAWL

(ANATOLY and FLORENCE are seen in their elevator.)

   FLORENCE.
I'M NOT GETTING RICH
MY ONLY INTEREST
IS IN SOMETHING WHICH
GIVES ME A CHANCE
OF WORKING WITH THE BEST
   ANATOLY.
I CAN ONLY SAY
I HOPE YOUR DREAM COMES TRUE
TILL THAT FAR-OFF DAY
I HOPE YOU COPE
WITH HELPING NUMBER TWO

FLORENCE &   **MOLOKOV &**
   ANATOLY.   **ARBITER.**
HOW SAD   IT'S VERY SAD TO SEE
TO SEE   THE ANCIENT AND
                         DISTINGUISHED GAME
                         THAT USED TO BE

ALL.
A MODEL OF DECORUM AND TRANQUILITY
BECOME LIKE ANY OTHER SPORT
A BATTLEGROUND FOR RIVAL IDEOLOGIES
TO SLUG IT OUT WITH GLEE

(ALL exit elevators and move to Arbiter's chambers.)

FLORENCE.	**ARBITER.**	**ANATOLY.**	**MOLOKOV.**
IT IS VERY SAD TO	IT'S SO SAD TO	SAD	HOW SAD
SEE	SEE A GAME THAT	IT IS VERY SAD TO	TO SEE
SAD TO SEE A	REALLY SHOULD	SEE	A DIS—
GAME THAT ONCE USED TO	BE	THIS DIS-TINGUISHED AND	TINGUISHED
BE A MODEL	LIKE A MODEL OF DE-CORUM	OLD GAME THAT	GAME THAT
OF CALM AND TRAN-		USED TO, THAT	ALWAYS
QUILITY	BECOME	USED TO BE TRAN-	USED TO BE
SAD WHEN IT BE-	JUST LIKE ANY OTHER	QUILITY	LIKE A
COMES LIKE ANY	SPORT A BATTLE-GROUND FOR	HAS BECOME	MODEL
OTHER SPORT	RIVAL IDE-	BATTLE-GROUND	OF DE-
JUST A BATTLE-	OLOGIES TO SLUG	SLUG IT OUT WITH GLEE	CORUM

GROUND, A BATTLE-	SLUG IT OUT	ANY OTHER SPORT	AND OF
GROUND FOR IDE-	SLUG IT OUT	LIKE A BATTLE- GROUND	PURE TRAN-
OLOGIES	IT IS VERY	SAD TO SEE	QUILITY
IT'S VERY SAD TO SEE THE ANCIENT	SAD SO SAD TO SEE	SO SAD	IT IS VERY SAD TO SEE THE
AND DISTIN- GUISHED GAME THAT	IT'S A	TO	OLD DISTIN- GUISHED GAME THAT
USED TO BE A	BATTLE- GROUND FOR	SEE A	USED TO BE
MODEL OF DECORUM	RIVAL IDE-	MODEL OF DECORUM	MODEL OF TRAN-
AND TRANQUILI TY BE-	OLOGIES	AND TRANQUILI TY	QUILITY
COME LIKE ANY OTHER	IT BECOMES	JUST LIKE ANY OTHER	WHEN IT BE-
SPORT	A BATTLE- GROUND FOR	SPORT HOW SAD	COMES A BATTLE-
LIKE A	IDEOLOGIES	TO SEE	GROUND THEN IT
BATTLE- GROUND FOR RIVAL	A BATTLE- GROUND	HOW THE GAME THAT	IS VERY
IDEOLOGIES	IT'S VERY SAD	USED TO BE	SAD, IT'S VERY SAD
IT'S VERY SAD	TO SEE A GAME	TRANQUILITY	WHEN THIS ANCIENT GAME BE-
SO SAD TO SEE	A BATTLE- GROUND	A BATTLE- GROUND	COMES A BATTLE- GROUND

ALL.
A PLACE TO SLUG IT OUT WITH GLEE.

(As song ends, all FOUR have arrived in the Arbiter's chambers.)

ARBITER. Mr. Sergievsky, you wouldn't consider abstaining from yogurt—

MOLOKOV. Are you suggesting—?

ARBITER. I'm not suggesting anything—except that we continue on with this match.

ANATOLY. I will be in my room—packing. *(Turns to FLORENCE, shakes his head.)* Such a waste. *(He leaves.)*

ARBITER. *(To MOLOKOV.)* People have invested millions of dollars in us, Mr. Molokov. In chess.

MOLOKOV. This is not my problem.

A R B I T E R . It fucking well is! *(Turns to FLORENCE.)* So what do you suggest we do? Let it all collapse in just one day? Let selfishness dictate to us? *(Yells.)* Not while I'm the arbiter of this match!! *(Beat.)* This is the message I want you to get across. Tomorrow morning I expect to see two smiling players at the table. I'll amend that. I don't give a shit if they're smiling. I don't care if they're bleeding. Two warm bodies are what's required, that's all!

(He goes. MOLOKOV and FLORENCE alone. Pause.)

MOLOKOV. *(Shaking his head.)* Yogurt?

FLORENCE. Why wouldn't he let anyone see the yogurt?

MOLOKOV. *(Laughs.)* It would be funny if it weren't so serious. *(Beat.)* It is serious?

FLORENCE. I can't imagine Freddie playing without an apology.

MOLOKOV. Why can't this just be chess?

FLORENCE. *(Turns on him.)* You of all people have the nerve to ask that?!

MOLOKOV. Me? I'm a chess second.

FLORENCE. Bull shit. (*Beat.*) Don't you think we know who you work for Mr. Molokov? The State Department briefed us before we came here.

MOLOKOV. This still does not mean I am not in love with the game of chess.

FLORENCE. (*Laughs to herself.*) I'll bet you love all kinds of games.

MOLOKOV. Florence Vassy. Left Hungary 1956. Mother dead. Father lost, presumed dead. Brought up by a Lawrence Osborne, professor of ancient history, Yale University. We have been briefed about you as well. (*Beat.*) Miss Vassy, 1956 was a long time ago. In the Soviet Union we have already forgotten it.

FLORENCE. I haven't. I still feel everything.

MOLOKOV. My country was asked to help—

FLORENCE. Don't give me any more reasons to hate you, Mr. Molokov, the old reasons are enough.

(Short pause.)

MOLOKOV. All right; Trumper leaves, what does that get him? He won't get a second chance.

FLORENCE. Freddie walks now, he says he caught the commie cheating. Who won't believe him? He'll be a hero. I suspect he could run for office. (*Beat.*) What does your guy take back home. (*Beat.*) Tomorrow.

(Pause.)

MOLOKOV. Must the meeting be in public?
FLORENCE. The apology.
MOLOKOV. The discussion.

(Pause.)

FLORENCE. I see no need for more publicity.
MOLOKOV. (*Quickly.*) I suggest our hotel room then.

FLORENCE. Very funny.
MOLOKOV. I know a private place. A restaurant.
FLORENCE. I know restaurants as well.

(Pause.)

MOLOKOV. Let us choose at random then. I have a Bangkok food guide. (*Takes it out of his pocket.*)
FLORENCE. I have the same one. (*She takes hers out of her purse.*) We'll use mine.
MOLOKOV. They're the same.
FLORENCE. So there's no problem with using mine.
MOLOKOV. I open, you point.
FLORENCE. (*Short pause. She thinks about this.*) Agreed.

(He opens. She points, but before they look:)

MOLOKOV. Let's make it the third below the one you've touched.
FLORENCE. The fourth.
BOTH. The second. (*Beat.*)
MOLOKOV/FLORENCE. *(Simultaneously.)* Agreed/Okay.
MOLOKOV. (*Reads.*) "The Generous Sole Bar."
FLORENCE. Sounds ideal.

End of Scene

ACT I

Scene 6

Freddie's suite. WALTER is on the phone.

WALTER. (*Into phone.*) A lot of nerve those guys have; yogurt, think of it! Nothing's sacred. I tell you they can't play chess without cheating. It's their nature. Freddie's completely disillusioned. He came here to play chess.

FLORENCE. (*Entering from the hall.*) Where's Freddie?

WALTER. Sh-sh. (*Into phone.*) Right. I think there's the point.

(*FLORENCE goes into bedroom.*)

WALTER. If you can't trust the Russians over chess—over a game—how the hell are you going to trust them with say an arms control deal? I mean that is basic common sense. But then what do I know?

FLORENCE. (*Coming out of the bedroom.*) Where is he?!

WALTER. (*Covering the speaker.*) Shut up. (*Into phone.*) I mean it, what do I know. I used to be a liberal myself, but that was back in the Sixties—

(*FLORENCE presses down the buttons on the phone, disconnecting him.*)

WALTER. (*Yells.*) What the hell are you doing?! That was the L.A. Times!!!

FLORENCE. Where did he go?

WALTER. It took me twenty minutes to make that connection. (*Starts to dial again.*)

FLORENCE. God damnit, tell me!!!

(*Short pause.*)

WALTER. (*Hangs up the phone.*) How the hell should I know where Freddie is? You're the nursemaid, I thought. Maybe he got tired of being treated like he didn't know anything—

FLORENCE. Who are you?

WALTER. What?

FLORENCE. What do you really want with Freddie?

WALTER. I want him to be rich. (*Beat.*) To recognize his potential. Chess games come and chess games go, but money—

FLORENCE. Why do I not believe this? (*Beat.*) What he did today is not his style.

WALTER. Walking out of a chess match is not Freddie Trumper's style? (*Laughs, takes out a cigarette.*) You're not suggesting *I* had anything to do with today?

FLORENCE. You follow the slime, you find the slug.

FREDDIE. (*Is seen standing at the door to the hallway. Holding up brochures.*) Wouldn't want to go home without seeing some of the sights. (*Reads.*) Patpong Palace. Sugar Shack. Girls Girls Girls. Ever been there, Walter?

WALTER. That's not something you confess to in front of a lady. (*He laughs and winks.*)

FLORENCE. (*To WALTER.*) Get out of here.

(*He looks to FREDDIE. Short pause.*)

FREDDIE. (*Looking through the brochures.*) You want to come, Florence? Could be a real education. (*Beat.*) Walter. (*Nods toward the door.*)

WALTER. (*To FLORENCE as he leaves.*) See. *He's* the boss. I'll be in my room. (*He goes.*)

FREDDIE. What if I told you—today was all my idea.

FLORENCE. Then I'd say—it was the first time you ever did something like that without talking it over with me.

FREDDIE. What if I said—I did it spontaneously?

FLORENCE. To that I'd say—only bad chess players move spontaneously. And that is one thing you are not.

FREDDIE. (*Turns away.*) I think making the point about Russians cheating is worthwhile in itself.

FLORENCE. Since when?!!! (*Pause. She hands him a piece of paper.*) Here, we're meeting Sergievsky at this restaurant at ten o'clock.

FREDDIE. He'll apologize?

FLORENCE. He'll meet us, that's enough.

FREDDIE. Not for me!

FLORENCE. (*Turns on him.*) What are you doing? This isn't the Freddie Trumper who lived just to play the game of chess!

FREDDIE. (*Turns on her, speaking over part of her line:*) Who was happy in ten-dollar shirts and playing chess games for the thrill of it?!!! (*Beat.*) You're right. (*Beat.*) I want to fulfill my potential.

FLORENCE. (*Disgusted.*) I wonder where you got that from.

FREDDIE. Florence, he wants to help me!

FLORENCE. Freddie, grow up!!!

FREDDIE. You work for me!!

[MUSIC #9: FLORENCE/AMERICAN]

[YOU WANNA LOSE YOUR ONLY FRIEND?]

FLORENCE. (*Sings out in anger.*)
YOU WANNA LOSE YOUR ONLY FRIEND?
WELL, KEEP IT UP YOU'RE DOING FINE
WHY THIS HUMILIATION?
WHY TREAT ME LIKE A FOOL?
I'VE TAKEN SHIT FOR SEVEN YEARS
AND I WON'T TAKE IT ANY MORE
    FREDDIE.
I'M ONLY TEASING SOVIETS
WITH GENTLE BONHOMIE
AND YOU'VE A BETTER REASON TO BE ANTI-
    THEM
THAN ME

FLORENCE.
THERE'S A TIME AND THERE'S A PLACE
   FREDDIE. Well how about here and now? Are you
for me or for them?
   FLORENCE.
THERE'S A TIME AND THERE'S A PLACE ...
   FREDDIE.
1956—BUDAPEST IS RISING
1956—BUDAPEST IS FIGHTING
1956—BUDAPEST IS FALLING
I'D HAVE THOUGHT YOU'D SUPPORT
ANY ATTACK ON THESE PEOPLE
ON THE PEOPLE WHO RAN
MINDLESS OVER YOUR CHILDHOOD
DON'T LET THEM FOOL YOU FOR
THIRTY YEARS ON THEY'RE THE SAME
   FLORENCE.
1956—BUDAPEST IS FIGHTING
1956—BUDAPEST IS DYING
   FREDDIE.
THEY SEE CHESS AS A WAR
PLAYING WITH PAWNS JUST LIKE POLAND
IF YOU WALK OUT ON ME
YOU'RE REALLY BETRAYING YOUR FATHER
WERE HE ALIVE NOW
HE'D SURELY BE DYING OF SHAME
   FLORENCE.
YOU KNOW THAT THERE'S NOTHING I'VE DONE
THAT HE'D BE ASHAMED OF IN MY WHOLE LIFE!
WHY'D YOU HAVE TO DO THIS TO ME?

(*FREDDIE storms out. FLORENCE runs to the door
   after him.*)

   FLORENCE. Where are you going, Freddie? Ten
o'clock! (*She runs back to gather her purse, and starts to
run after FREDDIE. She stops at the door again, and
comes back into the room. Pause. She sits and sings:*)

[MUSIC # 9A: SOMEONE ELSE'S STORY]

FLORENCE.
LONG AGO
IN SOMEONE ELSE'S LIFETIME
SOMEONE WITH MY NAME
WHO LOOKED A LOT LIKE ME
CAME TO KNOW
A MAN AND MADE A PROMISE
HE ONLY HAD TO SAY
AND THAT'S WHERE SHE WOULD BE
LATELY
ALTHOUGH HER FEELINGS RUN JUST AS DEEP
THE PROMISE SHE MADE HAS GROWN
   IMPOSSIBLE
TO KEEP
AND YET I WISH IT WASN'T SO
WILL HE MISS ME IF I GO?

IN A WAY
IT'S SOMEONE ELSE'S STORY
I DON'T SEE MYSELF
AS TAKING PART AT ALL
YESTERDAY
A GIRL THAT I WAS FOND OF
FINALLY COULD SEE THE WRITING ON THE
   WALL
SADLY
SHE REALIZED SHE'D LEFT HIM BEHIND
AND SADDER THAN THAT SHE KNEW HE
   WOULDN'T
EVEN MIND
AND THOUGH THERE'S NOTHING LEFT TO SAY
WOULD HE LISTEN IF I STAY

IT'S ALL VERY WELL TO SAY YOU FOOL IT'S
   NOW OR NEVER

I COULD BE CHOOSING
NO CHOICES WHATSOEVER

I COULD BE
IN SOMEONE ELSE'S STORY
IN SOMEONE ELSE'S LIFE
AND HE COULD BE IN MINE
I DON'T SEE
A REASON TO BE LONELY
I COULD TAKE MY CHANCES
FURTHER DOWN THE LINE
AND IF THAT GIRL I KNEW SHOULD ASK MY
    ADVICE
OH I WOULDN'T HESITATE SHE
NEEDN'T ASK ME TWICE
GO NOW!
I'D TELL HER THAT FOR FREE
TROUBLE IS, THE GIRL IS ME
THE STORY IS, THE GIRL IS ME

End of Scene

ACT I

Scene 7

[MUSIC # 10 GOLDEN BANGKOK] *The streets of Bangkok. FREDDIE, enjoying the sights of the town.*

[MUSIC # 10A: ONE NIGHT IN BANGKOK]

FREDDIE.
BANGKOK, ORIENTAL SETTING
AND THE CITY DON'T KNOW WHAT THE CITY IS
    GETTING
THE CREME DE LA CREME OF THE CHESS
    WORLD IN A

SHOW WITH EVERYTHING BUT YUL BRYNNER

BANGKOK, JUST ANOTHER STOP IN
THE CHESS WORLD CIRCUS—MASTERS DROP
IN,
PLAY, CHECKMATE, CHECK OUT AND THEN
YOU
MOVE ON TO ANOTHER VENUE

LIKE ICELAND—OR THE PHILIPPINES—OR
HASTINGS—OR—OR THIS PLACE!
CHORUS.
ONE NIGHT IN BANGKOK AND THE WORLD'S
YOUR OYSTER
THE BARS ARE TEMPLES BUT THE PEARLS AIN'T
FREE
YOU'LL FIND A GOD IN EVERY GOLDEN
CLOISTER
AND IF YOU'RE LUCKY THAN THE GOD'S A SHE
I CAN FEEL AN ANGEL IS SLIDING UP TO ME
FREDDIE.
ONE TOWN'S VERY LIKE ANOTHER
WHEN YOUR HEAD'S DOWN OVER YOUR PIECES,
BROTHER
CHORUS.
IT'S A DRAG, IT'S A BORE, IT'S REALLY SUCH A
PITY
TO BE LOOKING AT THE BOARD, NOT LOOKING
AT THE CITY
FREDDIE.
WHADDYA MEAN? YOU'VE SEEN ONE CROWDED,
POLLUTED, STINKING TOWN, YOU'VE SEEN—
CHORUS.
TEA, GIRLS, WARM, SWEET
SOME ARE SET UP IN THE SOMERSET MAUGHAN
SUITE
FREDDIE.
GET THAT! YOU'RE TALKING TO A TOURIST

WHOSE EVERY MOVE'S AMONG THE PUREST

I GET MY KICKS ABOVE THE WAISTLINE,
   SUNSHINE
CHORUS.
ONE NIGHT IN BANGKOK MAKES A HARD MAN
   HUMBLE
NOT MUCH BETWEEN DESPAIR AND ECSTASY
ONE NIGHT IN BANGKOK AND THE TOUGH
   GUYS TUMBLE
CAN'T BE TOO CAREFUL WITH YOUR COMPANY
I CAN FEEL THE DEVIL WALKING NEXT TO ME
   FREDDIE.
SIAM'S GONNA BE THE WITNESS
TO THE ULTIMATE TEST OF CEREBRAL FITNESS
THIS GRIPS ME MORE THAN WOULD A
MUDDY OLD RIVER OR RECLINING BUDDAH

I DON'T SEE YOU GUYS RATING
THE KIND OF MATE I'M CONTEMPLATING
I'D LET YOU WATCH, I WOULD INVITE YOU
BUT THE QUEENS WE USE WOULD NOT EXCITE
   YOU

SO YOU CAN KEEP YOUR BARS, YOUR TEMPLES,
   YOUR
MASSAGE PARLOURS ...
   CHORUS.
ONE NIGHT IN BANGKOK MAKES A HARD MAN
   HUMBLE
NOT MUCH BETWEEN DESPAIR AND ECSTASY
   FREDDIE. (*Spoken during instrumental break*.)
What was that place? The Generous Sole? The hell with
it.

(*INSTRUMENTAL*)

CHORUS.
ONE NIGHT IN BANGKOK AND THE WORLD'S
  YOUR OYSTER
THE BARS ARE TEMPLES BUT THE PEARLS AIN'T
  FREE
YOU'LL FIND A GOD IN EVERY GOLDEN
  CLOISTER
A LITTLE FLESH, A LITTLE HISTORY
I CAN FEEL AN ANGEL SLIDING UP TO ME

ONE NIGHT IN BANGKOK MAKES A HARD MAN
  HUMBLE
NOT MUCH BETWEEN DESPAIR AND ECSTASY
ONE NIGHT IN BANGKOK AND THE TOUGH
  GUYS TUMBLE
CAN'T BE TOO CAREFUL WITH YOUR COMPANY
I CAN FEEL THE DEVIL WALKING NEXT TO ME

[MUSIC #10B: BANGKOK—PLAYOFF]

ACT I

Scene 8

*Generous Sole Restaurant. ANATOLY and MOLOKOV
at a table. At some distance a MAN sits at another table
and eats.*

ANATOLY. So where is he?
MOLOKOV. I don't know. (*Mostly to himself.*)
Who'd ever think a game could get so complicated.
FLORENCE. (*Hurries in. Sees them, pretends to be
surprised.*) Oh hello! What a coincidence. We must have
the same Good Food Guide.
MOLOKOV. Of course you know—
FLORENCE. Yes. Hello.

MOLOKOV. Do you mind if she joins us?

FLORENCE. I wouldn't want to be in—

ANATOLY. Where's Trumper? Molokov told me why we're here.

FLORENCE. I don't know where he is.

MOLOKOV. Why the hell not?

FLORENCE. He's probably out with his agent.

MOLOKOV. Anderson. Yes, yes, I know him.

FLORENCE. How do you know him?

MOLOKOV. Our paths keep crossing.

ANATOLY. I told Molokov he wouldn't apologize.

FLORENCE. Freddie? *He* was going to apologize to *you*?

MOLOKOV. Maybe I can trace him. I shall need to make a call or two. If you would excuse me. (*He gets up and leaves.*)

FLORENCE. (*As he goes.*) How can you—? (*Beat. To ANATOLY.*) You have someone following Freddie?

ANATOLY. I don't. (*Beat.*) Don't you have someone who follows me?

FLORENCE. No. Of course not. You don't think I'm—

ANATOLY. No. Of course not. (*Awkward pause. He turns to the MAN at the other table, in Russian:*) How's the fish? *Cock REE-bah*?

MAN. (*In Russian.*) Excellent. *Ot-LEECH-nai-yah.*

FLORENCE. He's with you?

ANATOLY. I guess so.

FLORENCE. Then why is he sitting—? (*She stops herself.*)

ANATOLY. You cannot always choose—

BOTH. Who you work for. (*Beat.*)

FLORENCE. I can. (*Takes the bottle of wine.*) Do you mind if I—?

ANATOLY. Let me. (*Pours her a glass of wine.*) You're leaving Trumper?

FLORENCE. I didn't say that. I shouldn't have said anything.

ANATOLY. Someone like you—You could do better.

FLORENCE. What do you mean—"someone like you"? How do you know what I'm like?! (*Short pause.*) I'm sorry. Let's not argue.

ANATOLY. I don't want that.

FLORENCE. Neither do I. (*Awkward pause.*) Are you married?

ANATOLY. In a manner of speaking.

FLORENCE. Oh, I see.

ANATOLY. I doubt if you do.

FLORENCE. I didn't mean to suggest—

ANATOLY. I thought we weren't going to argue.

FLORENCE. That's true. So—we won't argue.

MAN. (*In Russian to ANATOLY.*) Do you have any salt? *Ooh vas YEST soil?*

FLORENCE. What did he say?

ANATOLY. He said you have lovely eyes.

FLORENCE. He said that? He can't even see my—

MAN. (*In Russian, repeats.*) Do you have any salt? *Ooh vas YEST soil?*

(*ANATOLY picks up a salt shaker, the MAN crosses to get the sale from him. Short pause.*)

FLORENCE. He asked for the salt?

[MUSIC #11: TERRACE DUET]

(*He nods. She laughs. He laughs, then looks at her.*)

FLORENCE. (*Stands up.*) Perhaps Freddie's on the terrace, excuse me. (*She goes onto the terrace. He watches her from the door.*)

[TERRACE DUET]

FLORENCE.
THIS IS THE ONE SITUATION
I WANTED MOST TO AVOID
NOTHING I SAY WILL CONVINCE HIM THIS ISN'T
   A TRICK
   ANATOLY.
A DRINK ON A CLEAR MOONLIT NIGHT—
I RELAX, SHE SMILES
THERE'S SOMETHING PECULIAR GOING ON
   FLORENCE.
SO, THROUGH NO FAULT OF MY OWN,
I'M IN IT WAY OVER MY HEAD.
EMBARRASSED, OUTNUMBERED, MAROONED
   ANATOLY.
NOW SHE CAN'T BE WORKING FOR THEM—
I MEAN US—!
SHE SEEMS TO KNOW WHAT SHE'S DOING—
BUT WHERE IS HE?
   FLORENCE.
HE HAS TO SHOW UP.
IT CAN'T COME TO NOTHING.
PERHAPS IT CAN.
   ANATOLY.
MAYBE HE'S SCARED—
BUT HE DIDN'T SEEM SCARED IN THE GAME
   FLORENCE.
OH, I JUST COULDN'T CARE LESS
HE CAN GO RIGHT AHEAD,
GO AND WRECK HIS CAREER,
I KNOW I'VE DONE MY BEST
   ANATOLY.
WELL AT LEAST SHE'S A GOOD-LOOKING SPY
   FLORENCE.
WHAT IF MY RUSSIAN FRIEND THINKS
THAT MY PLANS HAVE NOTHING TO DO WITH
   THE CHESS.
IF I DON'T SAY SOMETHING AND SOON
HE'LL GO—MAYBE I'M ON NOBODY'S SIDE

(*ANATOLY and FLORENCE on the terrace.*)

ANATOLY.
LISTEN, I HATE TO BREAK UP THE MOOD
HOW DO YOU SAY, BEGIN THE BEGUINE
HAVEN'T YOU NOTICED
WE'RE STILL ONE CHARACTER SHORT
IN THIS IDYLLIC, WELL-PRODUCED SCENE?
　　FLORENCE.
HOW COULD I NOT, MISS VASSY REGRETS
ANYTHING GOES, WITH YOUR OPPONENT
　　ANATOLY.
NEVER MIND HIM—I HAVEN'T MISSED HIM SO
　　FAR

(*Light-heartedly.*)

MAYBE IT WON'T DO ANY HARM
TO STRUGGLE ON WITHOUT HIS CHARM

(*More seriously.*)

FUNNY HOW ALL AT ONCE I FEEL
NOTHING ABOUT THAT MEETING MATTERS
　　ANYMORE
　　FLORENCE.
THIS IS THE ONE SITUATION
I WANTED MOST TO AVOID
　　ANATOLY.
MY DEAR OPPONENT—
I REALLY CAN'T IMAGINE WHY
　　FLORENCE.
YOU'LL THINK I'M THE DANGEROUS KIND—
WELL I AM!
　　ANATOLY.
YOU, YOU'RE NOT DANGEROUS—
WHO COULD THINK THAT OF YOU?

FLORENCE.
YOU—YOU ARE SO STRANGE—
WHY CAN'T YOU BE WHAT YOU OUGHT TO BE?
    FLORENCE & ANATOLY.
YOU SHOULD BE SCHEMING, INTRIGUING, TOO
CLEVER BY HALF
    ANATOLY.
I HAVE TO HAND IT TO YOU—
FOR YOU'VE MANAGED TO MAKE ME
FORGET WHY I EVER AGREED TO THIS FARCE.
    FLORENCE & ANATOLY.
I DON'T KNOW WHY I CAN'T THINK OF
ANYTHING
I WOULD RATHER DO
THAN BE WASTING MY TIME WITH SOMEONE
LIKE YOU.

(*As the song ends, they kiss.*)

    FLORENCE. This is insane.
    ANATOLY. Yes. It is. (*ANATOLY kisses her a second time.*) Can I see you again?

(*FLORENCE starts to kiss ANATOLY again. FREDDIE enters and sees them. He sings:*)

[WHO'D EVER THINK IT?]

    FREDDIE. (*Singing.*)
WHO'D EVER THINK IT?
SUCH A VERY PRETTY SETTING!
TELL ME WHAT'S THE BETTING
VERY PRETTY PLOTTING TOO?
NO MATTER—I'VE DONE ALL YOUR WORK FOR
YOU.
    (*Speaking.*) I asked you before—are you for me or for them? I think I know the answer!

FLORENCE. No, Freddie—
FREDDIE. Don't answer I think I know.

(*Singing.*)

WHO'D EVER GUESS IT?
DAUGHTER IN COLLABORATION
WITH THE VERY NATION
GAVE HER FATHER THIRD DEGREE!
WHERE'S DADDY? DEAD OR IN THE KGB?
    ANATOLY. Leave her alone, Trumper.
    MOLOKOV. (*Enters. In Russian, pulling ANATOLY away:*) I will handle this. *Ya EH-teem zai-MOOS.*
    ANATOLY. (*In Russian.*) Get away from me. *Ooh-I-DEE ot-S'YOO-dah.* (*Turns to FREDDIE.*) Trumper, I understand you came here to accept my apology.
    MOLOKOV. (*In Russian.*) Your apology? *Tee PRAW-zish- eez-vin-YEI-nee-ah?*
    ANATOLY. (*Ignoring him.*) In only a few minutes, Miss Vassy has made me realize how wrong I have been. What mistakes I have made. What I must change.
    FREDDIE. Forget it, Red. I don't need anything from you now. (*To FLORENCE.*) Walter was just telling me a group of fans phoned up and offered me another hundred grand to keep playing.
    WALTER. People love his style.
    FREDDIE. (*To WALTER.*) Tell them I accept. For a hundred grand, I guess I can sit there and hold my nose.
    MOLOKOV. Wonderful! We've made up! (*In Russian.*) You should get some sleep. *Ti-BYEH NAH-de bwee pah-SPAT.*
    WALTER. (*Who has watched this at some distance.*) You wanted groveling, you got groveling.
    MOLOKOV. (*In Russian.*) You can explain this when we get back. *Tee m'nyeh ah-b'yas-NEESH pah-TOME, v'gah-STEEN-it-s'yah.*

ANATOLY. (*In Russian.*) I have nothing to explain! *M'nyah N'YEH-che-vo ah-b'yas-N'YAT!*
FREDDIE. (*Turns to FLORENCE.*) You coming?

(She hesitates, then shakes her head; he looks at ANATOLY.)

ANATOLY. (*To FLORENCE.*) We could take you—
FLORENCE. No. (*Beat.*) Both of you—go, you need your rest.

End of Scene

ACT I

Scene 9

[MUSIC #12: CHESS #2]

Arena and later Florence's hotel room. CHESS MUSIC. FREDDIE and ANATOLY at chess board again. After a short while, ANATOLY makes a move. Pause. FREDDIE concedes. APPLAUSE. ANATOLY stands.

ARBITER. Mr. Sergievsky now leads three points to one. We adjourn until 10 o'clock tomorrow when we resume with the final game of the Bangkok portion of the World Chess Championship.

Gaw-spuh-DEEN Sergievsky vee-DYAWT suh-SH'YAW-tom tree-ah-DEEN. ZAF-truh VDY'EAH-sit cha-SAWF ooh-TRA su-stai-EET-s'ya fi-NAHL-nee-eh ee-GRA P"YER-voi puh-la-VEE-nee MEZH-doo-nah-RAWD-nuh-va Cham-pee-uh-NAH-ta SHAKH-mot-no-va v'Ban-KOK-yah.

Monsieur Sergievsky mene maintenant par trois points a un. Nous arretons le match et il reprendra demain a dix heures pour la final de la partie Bangkok du Tournois d'echecs mondial.

Herr Sergievsky fuhrt jetzt drei zu eims. Wir Brechen ab bis zehn uhr morgen wenn wir mit dem letzten spiel von dem Bangkok weitermachen werden.

(Various friends congratulate ANATOLY—in Russian. They pat his back, etc. During this time, ANATOLY looks over to FLORENCE. She looks at him. He moves towards her, but is unable to say anything because of FREDDIE's presence.)

NIKOLAI. (*In Russian.*) Come on, I think we've all deserved a drink. *Sta-REEK, NAH-da pah-ee-TEE VWEE-pit.*

(His friends pull him and they go off. The CROWD in the arena has left or is leaving. FLORENCE starts to go, then turns back and slowly goes up to FREDDIE who is still bent over the chess table, going over the last game)

FLORENCE. (*Trying to be friendly.*) That was a pretty foolish move you made in that game, Mr. Trumper. (*Beat.*) But we can all make foolish moves at times.

[MUSIC #13: FLORENCE QUITS]

(He looks at her, then turns on her, singing:)

[SO YOU GOT WHAT YOU WANT]

FREDDIE.
SO YOU GOT WHAT YOU WANT
WHAT A NASTY AMBITION!

SET ME UP, PULL ME DOWN
THEN EXPLOIT MY CONDITION

I SHOULD HAVE GUESSED, WOMAN
THAT IF PRESSED, WOMAN
YOU'RE ON NOBODY'S SIDE BUT YOUR OWN
AND YOU'RE BEHAVING
LIKE A MERE WOMAN
IT'S SO CLEAR, WOMAN—
IT'S YOUR SEX!
ONCE THEY START GETTING OLD AND GETTING
    WORRIED
THEY LET FLY, TAKE IT OUT
ON THE ONE THAT SUPPORTS THEM
THAT'S YOU THAT I'M TALKING ABOUT
    FLORENCE.
WHO'D EVER GUESS IT?
SUCH A SQUALID LITTLE ENDING
WATCHING YOU DESCENDING
JUST AS FAR AS YOU CAN GO
I'M LEARNING THINGS I DIDN'T WANT TO
    KNOW
    FREDDIE.
WHO'D EVER THINK IT?
THIS WOULD BE THE SITUATION—
ONE MORE OBSERVATION—
HOW'D WE EVER GET THIS FAR
BEFORE YOU SHOWED ME WHAT YOU REALLY
    ARE?
    FLORENCE.
YOU'LL BE LOST WITHOUT ME
TO ABUSE LIKE YOU'RE USED TO
    FREDDIE.
GO AWAY! JUST GET US OUT!
BE SOMEONE ELSE'S PARASITE!

[MUSIC #13A: A TASTE OF PITY]

I'M NOT THE KIND TO BE VINDICTIVE
HOLDING SOME CHILDISH GRUDGE
HOW COULD I BE? I'M IN THE SPOTLIGHT
HALF OF THE WORLD MY JUDGE
ALL I DEMAND IS THOSE I WORK FOR
THOSE I GIVE ALL MY SKILLS, ALL MY TIME
  AND PAIN
THOSE THAT I ENTERTAIN
GIVE ME THE SAME COMPASSION IN RETURN
BUT YOUR KIND NEVER LEARN!

(*He exits.*)

[MUSIC # 14: NOBODY'S SIDE]

FLORENCE.
WHAT'S GOING ON AROUND ME
IS BARELY MAKING SENSE
I NEED SOME EXPLANATIONS FAST
I SEE MY PRESENT PARTNER
IN THE IMPERFECT TENSE
AND I DON'T SEE HOW WE CAN LAST
I FEEL I NEED A CHANGE OF CAST
MAYBE I'M ON NOBODY'S SIDE

AND WHEN HE GIVES ME REASONS
TO JUSTIFY EACH MOVE
THEY'RE GETTING HARDER TO BELIEVE
I KNOW THIS CAN'T CONTINUE
I'VE STILL A LOT TO PROVE
THERE MUST BE MORE I COULD ACHIEVE
BUT I DIDN'T HAVE THE NERVE TO LEAVE

EVERYBODY'S PLAYING THE GAME
BUT NOBODY'S RULES ARE THE SAME
NOBODY'S ON NOBODY'S SIDE
BETTER LEARN TO GO IT ALONE
RECOGNIZE YOU'RE OUT ON YOUR OWN

NOBODY'S ON NOBODY'S SIDE

*(The scene changes to Florence's hotel room. As she
packs her clothes in a suitcase.)*

FLORENCE.
THE ONE I SHOULD NOT THINK OF
KEEPS ROLLING THROUGH MY MIND
AND I DON'T WANT TO LET THAT GO
NO LOVER'S EVER FAITHFUL
NO CONTRACT TRULY SIGNED
THERE'S NOTHING CERTAIN LEFT TO KNOW
AND HOW THE CRACKS BEGIN TO SHOW!

NEVER MAKE A PROMISE OR PLAN
TAKE A LITTLE LOVE WHERE YOU CAN
NOBODY'S ON NOBODY'S SIDE
NEVER STAY TOO LONG IN YOUR BED
NEVER LOSE YOUR HEART, USE YOUR HEAD
NOBODY'S ON NOBODY'S SIDE

NEVER TAKE A STRANGER'S ADVICE
NEVER LET A FRIEND FOOL YOU TWICE
NOBODY'S ON NOBODY'S SIDE
NEVER BE THE FIRST TO BELIEVE
NEVER BE THE LAST TO DECEIVE
NOBODY'S ON NOBODY'S SIDE
AND—
NEVER LEAVE A MOMENT TOO SOON
NEVER WASTE A HOT AFTERNOON
NOBODY'S ON NOBODY'S SIDE
NEVER STAY A MINUTE TOO LONG
DON'T FORGET THE BEST WILL GO WRONG
NOBODY'S ON NOBODY'S SIDE

BETTER LEARN TO GO IT ALONE
RECOGNIZE YOU'RE OUT ON YOUR OWN
NOBODY'S ON NOBODY'S SIDE

End of Scene

[MUSIC #14A: NOBODY'S—PLAYOFF]

Act I

Scene 10

Underground parking square below the arena. Sound of a CAR, LIGHTS sweep across the stage; sound of CAR DOORS. Echoed footsteps and then two MEN enter with FLORENCE. One MAN carries her suitcase, the OTHER has his hand under her elbow.

1st MAN. (*To 2ND MAN.*) We'll wait here.

(*2ND MAN who has the luggage, starts to go.*)

FLORENCE. You going to take my luggage with you?

(*He comes back and sets the suitcase down and then leaves.*)

FLORENCE. (*To 1ST MAN.*) My whole life's in there. (*Nods toward the suitcase.*) That says something about me, doesn't it? (*Tries to move her elbow.*) You're not going to let go, are you?
WALTER. (*Hurries in.*) It took you long enough.
1st MAN. Pete just—
WALTER. I ran into him on the stairs. I'll handle it.

(*1ST MAN goes.*)

FLORENCE. What do you have to do with this?

WALTER. Lucky for us your plane was delayed. You could have been on your way home

FLORENCE. Who are you Mr. Anderson? And what do you want with me?

WALTER. You just missed the Bangkok closing ceremonies. (*Takes out letter.*) Read this. It was addressed to you.

FLORENCE. And you opened it.

WALTER. Your friend should be happy I did. (*She reads.*) He played a beautiful game today. He seemed inspired. Poor Freddie. It's four to one now. (*Beat.*) Surprised? (*She is stunned.*)

(*In the background sound of another CAR, LIGHTS, etc. WALTER looks in that direction.*)

FLORENCE. I guess I am. (*Beat.*) Yes. Of course.

WALTER. You had no idea?

FLORENCE. There was only that one evening ... He knows nothing about me. (*Beat.*) I want to be with him.

WALTER. This will soon be arranged.

FLORENCE. When does it happen?

WALTER. Tonight. We need you to go to his room ...

(*An American REPORTER enters from his car. WALTER stops talking and steps out of sight behind a concrete column. REPORTER starts to walk by, but then notices FLORENCE.*)

REPORTER. Excuse me, aren't you with Mr. Trumper?

FLORENCE. I've been his second.

REPORTER. (*Walks to her, takes out pad and pencil.*) Couple of questions?

WALTER. (*Protecting her.*) What do you want?

REPORTER. (*Showing press pass.*) Associated Press. I just came from the airport and there a rumor there that Anatoly Sergievsky's about to defect—

(*WALTER grabs him by the collar and throws him against a wall. FLORENCE is stunned by this sudden violence.*)

WALTER. Listen, don't you say that to anyone!! You understand?! (*Slaps him.*) Do you understand?! (*REPORTER nods.*) We're talking about a man's life here! You moron. The ceremonies have been over five minutes now. Everyone should be on their way down. (*To FLORENCE.*) Don't move. (*To REPORTER.*) Stay right there. We better just get this over with!

(*WALTER goes. FLORENCE and the REPORTER look at each other both frightened. After a moment, a few AMERICANS hurry in from where Walter exited and rush across the garage. Sounds of CARS being started, squeal of BRAKES, sweep of LIGHTS. Suddenly ANATOLY, surrounded by AMERICANS who are protecting him, is rushed across the garage.*)

CIA MAN. (*As LIGHTS sweep across.*) What the hell—?
WALTER. It's us. It's us!!

(*ANATOLY is raced across the garage.*)

FLORENCE. Anatoly!
WALTER. (*Runs in and grabs FLORENCE.*) Come on. I said, come on!

(*He pulls her off in the direction that ANATOLY went. REPORTER runs off in other direction. Squeal of BRAKES. Suddenly NIKOLAI runs in, hears the sound of a CAR.*)

NIKOLAI. Sergievsky!!! (*CAR squeals. MOLOKOV and other RUSSIANS hurry in. MOLOKOV holds up his hand; the CAR turns the corner and appears to drive right at him.*)
MOLOKOV. Stop! Stop! Anatoly!!!

(*The CAR turns, squealing, and goes off in another direction.*)

MOLOKOV. Anderson, you bastard!!!

(*CAR squeals away.*)

End of Scene

ACT I

Scene Eleven

A small baggage room at the airport and later a concourse in the airport. ANATOLY and FLORENCE sit on separate trunks. Announcements, in Thai, heard over P.A. System.

ANATOLY. What's the delay?
WALTER. Five minutes. Relax. I'll have some food brought in. (*He goes. Pause.*)
FLORENCE. You don't have any children, do you?
ANATOLY. Just a wife. (*Beat.*)
FLORENCE. (*More to herself.*) Just a wife.
ANATOLY. She and I—
FLORENCE. Don't tell me.
ANATOLY. This—It affects nothing. (*Beat.*) It had already gone wrong between us.

FLORENCE. So at least I am not a homewrecker too. I mean as well as being a traitor to the man I've been working with for seven years.

ANATOLY. Just working with?

FLORENCE. This—it affects nothing. (*Beat.*)

ANATOLY. I am counting on your giving me inside information on his game—while we're in bed together.

FLORENCE. (*Smiles.*) Is that all you think about?

ANATOLY. Chess?

FLORENCE. (*Laughs.*) No.

(*HAROLD and JOE, two men from the Embassy enter with a pile of junk food that can be bought from machines.*)

JOE. Mr. Anderson said you were hungry.

FLORENCE. Thank you. (*Short pause.*)

HAROLD. Been to America before?

ANATOLY. No, no I haven't.

HAROLD. I think you'll like it. Most people do.

JOE. Though if it were up to me, I'd say choose the East, not the West. (*ANATOLY looks at him.*) East Coast, I mean. I'm from New York myself.

(*A MAN appears at the door.*)

THIRD MAN. Harold, Joe. (*They start to go.*)

HAROLD. Good luck. (*They go.*)

THIRD MAN. Relax!

FLORENCE. I hope you find America all it's cracked up to be.

ANATOLY. In the Soviet Union, it is not cracked up to be all that much.

FLORENCE. (*Smiles.*) Yes. (*Beat.*) I still don't feel completely at home, and I came there when I was—

ANATOLY. Florence. (*She turns to him.*) Please. I am scared enough.

(She suddenly realizes how frightened he must be.)

FLORENCE. Anatoly. (*She hugs him.*)

(Door opens. WALTER enters, followed by REPORTERS.)

WALTER. Line up there. Hurry, please. Time is short.
FLORENCE. (*Turns to WALTER.*) You said this would be private!
WALTER. Nothing's for free. (*He points to one of the REPORTERS yelling questions.*) You!
REPORTER. Mr. Sergievsky. Why now? Why under glasnost?
FLORENCE. Anatoly, don't answer—
ANOTHER REPORTER. Are you part of a political dissident movement—?
ANOTHER REPORTER. The American Embassy has put out a statement saying you have asked for political asylum—
ANOTHER REPORTER. Would you call yourself a political refugee?!!
ANATOLY. No, I am not a refugee!! You don't under—
ANOTHER REPORTER. Anatoly, is this your way of denouncing the Gorbachev—
ANATOLY. I denounce nothing!! Please understand that. (*Beat.*) I am not a politician.
FLORENCE. Anatoly—
ANATOLY. I would like to live in many places of the world. There are things I wish to do. Things I was not free to —

[MUSIC #17: REPORTERS]

CIA MAN. They're ready.

(FLORENCE and ANATOLY follow WATER out into the concourse, en route to the departure gates. REPORTERS follow, shouting (sung) questions.)

REPORTER.
HOW LONG WAS THIS PLANNED?
REPORTER.
WHAT MADE YOU DEFECT?
REPORTER.
DID ANYONE HELP YOU?
REPORTER.
AND DO YOU EXPECT
TO BE JOINED BY LOVED ONES
REPORTER.
SUCH AS YOUR WIFE
REPORTER.
OR ARE YOU STARTING AGAIN IN ALL ASPECTS
OF LIFE?
ANATOLY. You do not hear what I am saying. I do not leave.
REPORTER.
DO YOU STILL INTEND TO FINISH THE MATCH
REPORTER.
OR HAVE YOU RESIGNED NOW
ALL.
OR SHOULD WE ATTACH ANY SPECIAL
SIGNIFICANCE
TO YOUR PRETTY NEW FRIEND—
AND COULD THIS GREAT DECISION BE A START
OR AN END?
ANATOLY. *(At gates, as a REPORTER grabs his arm.)* Leave me alone!

[MUSIC # 17A: ANTHEM]

ANATOLY.
NO MAN, NO MADNESS
THOUGH THEIR SAD POWER MAY PREVAIL

CAN POSSESS, CONQUER, MY COUNTRY'S
  HEART
THEY RISE TO FAIL
SHE IS ETERNAL
LONG BEFORE NATIONS' LINES WERE DRAWN
WHEN NO FLAGS FLEW, WHEN NO ARMIES
  STOOD
MY LAND WAS BORN

AND YOU ASK ME WHY I LOVE HER
THROUGH WARS, DEATH AND DESPAIR
SHE IS CONSTANT, WE WHO DON'T CARE
AND YOU WONDER WILL I LEAVE HER—BUT
  HOW?
I CROSS OVER BORDERS BUT I'M STILL THERE
  NOW.

HOW CAN I LEAVE HER?
WHERE WOULD I START?
LET MAN'S PETTY NATIONS TEAR THEMSELVES
  APART
MY LAND'S ONLY BORDERS LIE AROUND MY
  HEART

End of Act I

ACT II

Scene 1

[MUSIC #18: BUDAPEST 1988]

Budapest, eight weeks later. Noise of the TRAFFIC from the street just offstage as a CHOIR sings a HUNGARIAN FOLK SONG. During the song, FLORENCE and ANATOLY enter with two AMERICANS.

[MUSIC # 19: HUNGARIAN FOLK SONG]

CHOIR.
MINDEN VAGYAM VISSZASZALL
ODA HOL AZ EDES HAZAM VAR
ZOLD ERDO VIRAGOS RET
SHAL A REGL REGL HAZAM MEG
TUDOM EGYSZER VISSZETEREK EN
VISSZA MEG, VISSZA MEG,
VISSZA MEG, VISSZA MEG,
BUJDOSASOM VEGET ER
S'ITT VAGOYOK UJRA
SZEP HAZAMBAN EN

(The CHOIR ends its song; the CONDUCTOR talks to individual members, giving them direction. FLORENCE claps.)

HUNGARIAN WOMAN. *(In Hungarian, to FLORENCE.)* Have you heard them sing in church? *Hallotiad oket epy templomban enokelai?*
FLORENCE. I don't—I— *(She turns to ANATOLY.)*

ANATOLY. I'm not the Hungarian.
FLORENCE. I am sorry, I don't understand. I am very sorry.

(WOMAN walks off, WALTER hurries in, smiling.)

WALTER. There you two are, welcome to Budapest! Forgive me for not meeting you myself. How do you like the hotel, quaint, isn't it?
FLORENCE. Our room is very light, thank you.
WALTER. *(Not listening to FLORENCE, to BEN.)* Any problems with customs?
BEN. They went right through.
WALTER. I tell you the world is awash with peace all of a sudden. Who'd have ever thought?
FLORENCE. *(She kisses ANATOLY on the cheek.)* I won't be long. *(She starts to leave, to WALTER.)* Beautiful choir. *(She leaves.)*
WALTER. Where's she—?
ANATOLY. She's excited. She wants to look around.
WALTER. And you aren't going with her?
ANATOLY. I thought—
WALTER. That someone would walk by and stab you with a poisoned umbrella tip? *(Laughs, puts his arm around ANATOLY.)*
CHOIR. *(Starts again, under dialogue.)*
NEM CSABIT A MESSZESEG
NEM CSABIT A NAGUYVLLAG
EIMULT MINEN KISERTESEM MAR

TUDOM ITTHON VAGYOK VEGRE MAR
VEGRE MAR
BUJDOAASOM BEGET ERT
S ITT VAGYOK VEGRE
     SZEP HAZAMBAN EN
WALTER. Relax, Anatoly, no one is going to hurt you here. Now forgive me again, but I've promised to

have a word with some people from State. You'll be interested to know, Anatoly, that the Secretary himself is looking forward to meeting you while he's here. I don't suppose that will be a problem. If it hadn't been for the Summit being here, you wouldn't have even been let in. And this may end up being its greatest accomplishment. (*He laughs and hurries off.*)

PETE. By the way (*Nods toward the choir.*) they were rehearsing for the Summit, not for your benefit.

ANATOLY. I didn't think—

BEN. Trumper did, didn't he? Trumper thinks everything's for him.

(*Along with the members of the choir and others, THREE RUSSIANS have entered. ONE suddenly runs toward ANATOLY.*)

1ST RUSSIAN. Tolya Sergievsky!

ANATOLY. Josef! (*To BEN and PETE.*) They are old friends from my town. (*In Russian, he greets them, then:*) What are you doing here? *Shtaw vivee toot D'YALE-ae-a-tyeh?*

(*There are greetings as they hug. Simultaneously.*)

ANATOLY. This is a great surprise! *Ka-KOY s'yur-PREES!* Which hotel are you in? *Fka-KOY vivee gah-STEEN-it-s'yah?*

1ST RUSSIAN. How are you? *Noo, COCK tee?* It's wonderful to see you! *Rad ti-BYAH VEE-dyet!* We were just talking about you! *Ah mwee TOIL-ka shte guh-vah-REEL-oe ah ti-BYEH!* He looks good! *Awh pri-KRAS-na VWEE-gli-dit!*

2ND RUSSIAN. We were hoping we'd run into you, Anatoly. *Mwee TOCK oe DOO-mah-lee shte FSTRAY-tim ti-BYAH.* How are you? *Cock ZHEEZN muh-la-DAI-a?* You haven't changed. *Tee sef-S'YEM nee*

eez-men-N' EEL-s'ye. We have tickets for your match.
Ah ooh nas YEST bil-YET-oe nah match.

PETE. (*As they go off, following ANATOLY and the RUSSIANS.*) Now, why would they give three old friends of a defector, permission to come to Hungary?

[MUSIC # 19A: HUNGARY—PLAYOFF]

End of Scene

ACT II

Scene 2

A chapel of a large Cathedral; rows of candles. FLORENCE is looking around. Short pause. From the shadows a figure appears; it is MOLOKOV.

MOLOKOV. Here to pray for victory, Miss Vassy? Or just sightseeing?

FLORENCE. (*Turns.*) Molokov? (*Beat.*) Are you following me now?

MOLOKOV. A coincidence. I love cathedrals. I love this cathedral. (*He goes to the candles.*) Who shall I pray for to win? The old American or the new American? (*Lights the candle.*) I think I shall pray that my wife stays faithful to me.

FLORENCE. What do you want, Molokov?

MOLOKOV. I am here for the chess. I have nothing else to do here. Mr. Anatoly Sergievsky has seen to that.

FLORENCE. It had nothing to do with you.

MOLOKOV. Miss Vassy, why did I not just say that to my superiors when I got home from Bangkok. Sirs, this defection, it had nothing to do with me. (*Pause. Sighs.*) You have a beautiful country here.

FLORENCE. This isn't my country.

MOLOKOV. No?

FLORENCE. I don't even speak the language. I'm a tourist. I have no memories of anything.

MOLOKOV. For that I am sorry.

(She turns to him, surprised by this remark.)

MOLOKOV. It's a charming city. My own honeymoon was here. *(Beat.)*

FLORENCE. I couldn't even find Prodgsy street where I was born. It's very near to here I know. *(Turns to him.)* I thought maybe there'd be neighbors who remembered ... *(Shrugs.)* What happened to my father.

MOLOKOV. Perhaps they changed the street names. *(Beat.)* I could ask. *(Beat.)* I speak some Hungarian.

FLORENCE. I wouldn't want you to go to any trouble—

MOLOKOV. It would be no trouble at all. *(He starts to go.)* By the way, I'm told Anatoly seems very very happy. No doubt, because of you. Feel complimented by that. *(Beat.)* My wife would. She would be very pleased to have that said about me. *(Beat.)* I've been a stupid husband, Florence. So much time away. She kept saying, if I loved her, I should give her every second. But I was young. *(He laughs and goes.)*

[MUSIC # 20: HEAVEN HELP MY HEART]

FLORENCE.
IF IT WERE LOVE I SHOULD GIVE THAT LOVE
EVERY SECOND I HAD
AND I DO
DID I KNOW WHERE HE'D LEAD ME TO?
DID I PLAN
DOING ALL OF THIS FOR THE LOVE OF A MAN?
WELL LET IT HAPPEN ANYHOW
AND WHAT I'M FEELING NOW
HAS NO EASY EXPLANATION

REASON PLAYS NO PART
HEAVEN HELP MY HEART
I LOVE HIM TOO MUCH
WHAT IF HE SAW MY WHOLE EXISTENCE
TURNING AROUND A WORD, A SMILE, A TOUCH?

ONE OF THESE DAYS, AND IT WON'T BE LONG,
HE'LL KNOW MORE ABOUT ME
THAN HE SHOULD
ALL MY DREAMS WILL BE UNDERSTOOD
NO SURPRISE
NOTHING MORE TO LEARN FROM THE LOOK IN
   MY EYES
THOUGH I KNOW THAT TIME IS NOT MY FRIEND
I'LL FIGHT IT TO THE END
HOPING TO KEEP THIS BEST OF MOMENTS
WHEN THE PASSIONS START
HEAVEN HELP MY HEART
THE DAY THAT I FIND
SUDDENLY I'VE RUN OUT OF SECRETS
SUDDENLY I'M NOT ALWAYS ON HIS MIND

MAYBE IT'S BEST TO LOVE A STRANGER
WELL THAT'S
WHAT I'VE DONE—
HEAVEN HELP MY HEART
HEAVEN HELP MY HEART

End of Scene

[MUSIC # 20A: HEAVEN—PLAYOFF]

ACT II

Scene 3

Freddie's suite. FREDDIE is in a chair across from an attractive female REPORTER, who sits on the couch, notebook in her lap, her legs crossed.

FEMALE REPORTER. What a beautiful suite! What do you think of Budapest so far, Mr. Trumper?

FREDDIE. Anyone with legs like that can call me Freddie. (*She uncrosses her legs.*) That's a joke, okay? (*He gets up.*) Jesus Christ, you been here how long? A couple of days! And already you've lost your sense of humor. See what Communism does to you? (*She smiles.*) Now there's a smile. You got a mouth like that, you should show it. Make people happy. So what was the question? Oh, Budapest, yeah. (*Beat.*) It stinks. You been outside? (*Beat.*) I have. Once. The goddamn Danube isn't even blue. (*She laughs.*) You write that down.

FEMALE REPORTER. I am. (*As she writes.*) And Mr. Sergievsky? Have you seen him yet?

FREDDIE. I see him in my dreams, honey.

FEMALE REPORTER. I mean in person. He's staying in the hotel.

(Short pause.)

FREDDIE. That, I wasn't told.

WALTER. (*Enters.*) Freddie, excuse me, the Secretary of State—

FREDDIE. Fuck the Secretary of State. You're interrupting, Walter. This young woman from ...?

FEMALE REPORTER. Tennessee.

FREDDIE. Tennessee. She's been drawing me out, Walter. She's getting me to reveal things about myself I never even knew.

WALTER. Good for her, but—

FREDDIE. And she's been telling me things I was never told before. Like—Sergievsky's in this hotel.

WALTER. That's true. There's only one deluxe—

FREDDIE. And is his bitch with him?

(Pause. WALTER crosses to the REPORTER.)

WALTER. If you'd excuse us please—

FEMALE REPORTER. We haven't finished—

WALTER. Just call and we'll arrange another time.

FEMALE REPORTER. *Vanity Fair* needs the story in—

WALTER. I said just call. (*He has led her out the door. He turns back to FREDDIE. Short pause.*) Florence is here. Yes.

FREDDIE. Good. Maybe she'll exhaust him. Like rabbits, that's how I bet they are.

WALTER. Freddie, there's the Secretary of State—

FREDDIE. She screwing him too?

(He laughs. WALTER doesn't.)

WALTER. He wants to come and watch a game. While he's here at—

FREDDIE. I don't need that kind of distraction.

WALTER. He'd come with what? Five, six others. I'll keep it down. It'd be no big thing. (*Beat.*) If I hadn't told you—

FREDDIE. *Asked* me. You *ask* me, remember? (*Beat.*) I tell *you.* (*Beat.*) This Summit's caused me enough trouble already without messing up the match. Look at the room I get.

WALTER. It is the best hotel room in Budapest. The president of the United States doesn't have a room as good.

FREDDIE. Yeah? (*Beat.*) Is it the best room in this hotel?

WALTER. It's the best room on the goddamn earth. (*Beat.*) Freddie, the Secretary comes to the match, gets his picture taken shaking hands with an authentic American genius. What's the big deal?

FREDDIE. I don't let myself be used like that.

WALTER. You've been used like that a hundred times!!

FREDDIE. (*Yelling.*) I haven't, Walter!! I've been very careful, I've been my own man!!

WALTER. What's one goddamn picture?!!

FREDDIE. You tell the Secretary of State that I am very busy and that he can (go fuck himself!!) [or alternative line—kiss my ass!!]

(*Beat.*)

WALTER. Okay. I'll tell him. (*Beat.*) Maybe not in those exact words—

FREDDIE. And you can tell those two commies in heat that we may be in the same hotel but they better stay out of my way. (*Beat.*) If I'd known I'd have asked for a place a little less polluted—like the gutter.

[MUSIC # 21: WINNING]

WALTER.
YOU TAKE CARE YOU DON'T LET
THEIR SHENNANIGANS BLIND YOU
AND YOU'RE WRONG TO FORGET
YOU'VE GOT YOUR COUNTRY BEHIND YOU
    FREDDIE.
YOU'RE A FOOL IF YOU THINK YOU CAN WAVE
    A FLAG
AND INSPIRE SOME DRAMATIC ACTION
IF I WANT BAD ENOUGH THEN IT'S IN THE BAG
IF I DON'T YOU'RE A MERE DISTRACTION
    WALTER.
YOU TAUGHT ME BABY

HOW THE FEW WHO WIN ACQUIRE
WHAT THEIR HEARTS DESIRE
IT AIN'T PRACTICE, IT AIN'T SKILL
THEY'LL HELP BUT NOT AS MUCH AS WANTING
   WILL
   FREDDIE.
NO CONTEST BABY
PAY NO MIND TO REPUTATION
YOU WANT CONCENTRATION?
WHEN THEY PICK HIM OFF THE FLOOR
IT'S CAUSE I WANTED IT A LITTLE MORE
   WALTER.
YOU CAN WIN YOU CAN LOSE
TAKE OR BE A POSSESSION
YOU TAUGHT ME HOW TO CHOOSE
AND THE KEY IS OBSESSION
   FREDDIE.
SEE MY EYES, ARE THEY SAFE ARE THEY EVEN
   SANE?
ARE THEY WARM WHEN THEY SEEM TO GREET
   YOU?
YOU DON'T KNOW, YOU CAN'T TELL, BUT IT
   SHOULD BE PLAIN
THESE ARE EYES THAT ARE GONNA BEAT YOU
DON'T EVER TELL ME
I DON'T KNOW THE WAY TO PLAY IT
DO I HAVE TO SAY IT?
DOESN'T MATTER WHAT HE TRIES,
I HAVE HIM, YOU CAN SEE IT IN THE EYES
   BOTH.
NO CONTEST BABY
BARELY ANY POINT IN PLAYING
WHEN IT'S JUST DELAYING
WHAT WE BOTH ALREADY KNOW
HE LOST IT A WOMAN AND A HALF AGO

HE LOST IT A WOMAN AND A HALF AGO
                End of Scene

ACT II

Scene 4

A walk along the Danube; ANATOLY, FLORENCE, and the three RUSSIANS from the lobby. Evening, after dinner. They are saying goodbye.

ALEXI. (*In Russian.*) Seriously, you've never played better. *Si-ree-AWZ-na, tee nee-tog-DAH tak khuh-rah-shaw nee au-GRAL.*

ANATOLY. (*To FLORENCE.*) Alexi says this afternoon was the best he'd ever seen me play.

3RD RUSSIAN. (*In Russian.*) You're in good form, no worse than in Bangkok. *Tee FFORM-ya, nee KHOO-zhe chem v Ban-COCK-ya.*

ANATOLY. (*To FLORENCE.*) That I've lost nothing since Bangkok.

FLORENCE. Why should you have—?

2ND RUSSIAN. (*In Russian.*) It's only a matter of days before you finish with the American. *Ooh-VYARE-an, CHI-raz PAH-roo DNYEI tee ah-bi-GRAI-esh Ah-mer-i-KAN-sa.*

ANATOLY. (*In Russian.*) We can hope. *BOO-dyem nah-DYEI-it-s'ya.* (*To FLORENCE.*) That I could be finished with Freddie in a few days.

1ST RUSSIAN. (*In Russian, to FLORENCE.*) Thank you. *Spah-SEE-ba.* (*They shake hands.*)

FLORENCE. It was a pleasure.

(THE RUSSIANS exchange goodbyes and walk off in one direction. FLORENCE and ANATOLY look over the river.)

FLORENCE. They're very nice.

ANATOLY. I'm sorry if we talked so much in Russian.

FLORENCE. Please. I understand. They're your friends.

ANATOLY. They don't speak any English.

FLORENCE. It was nice to see you enjoying yourself.

ANATOLY. Since Bangkok when have you not seen me enjoying myself?

FLORENCE. (*Smiles.*) I meant—with others. With friends.

ANATOLY. Ah.

FLORENCE. There was someone that you all kept talking about, a "Svetlana." (*Beat.*) I think Svetlana. I didn't understand. What any of you were saying. (*Beat.*) "Svetlana"'something. "Svetlana" something else. (*Beat.*) Didn't you tell me your wife's name is Svetlana?

ANATOLY. Florence!

FLORENCE. Your wife? That Svetlana? That's who you were talking about?

ANATOLY. Yes. (*Beat.*) She's here. In Budapest.

FLORENCE. (*Taken aback.*) Oh.

ANATOLY. Molokov, no doubt …

FLORENCE. Yes. No doubt. (*Beat.*) Maybe.

ANATOLY. Beautiful night.

FLORENCE. Every night's been beautiful for two months. Are you going to see her?

ANATOLY. Should I?

FLORENCE. This is your move, Anatoly, not mine.

ANATOLY. We aren't playing a game of chess, Florence.

FLORENCE. Move.

ANATOLY. If you don't want me to see her …

FLORENCE. What I want can have nothing to do with this. If I say no—(*Beat.*) I don't want you to resent me either.

ANATOLY. I don't love her.

FLORENCE. You married her.

ANATOLY. Years ago.

FLORENCE. And years ago you loved her.

[MUSIC # 22: YOU AND I]

FLORENCE.
THIS IS AN ALL TOO FAMILIAR SCENE
LIFE IMPERCEPTIBLY COMING BETWEEN
THOSE WHOSE LOVE IS AS STRONG AS IT COULD
  OR SHOULD BE
  ANATOLY.
NOTHING HAS ALTERED—
  FLORENCE.
—YET EVERYTHING'S CHANGED
  ANATOLY.
NO ONE STANDS STILL—
  BOTH.
STILL I LOVE YOU COMPLETELY AND HOPE I
  ALWAYS WILL
  ANATOLY.
WHY DO WE NEED TO PUT LOVE INTO WORDS?
CAUSING
CONFUSION
WE PROTECT, EXPLAIN
REASSURE, IN VAIN
COME TO NO CONCLUSION
  FLORENCE.
I'D GIVE THE WORLD TO STAY JUST AS WE ARE
IT'S BETTER BY FAR
NOT TO BE TOO WISE
NOT TO REALIZE
  BOTH.
WHERE THERE'S TRUTH THERE WILL BE LIES
  FLORENCE.
YOU AND I
  BOTH.
WE'VE SEEN IT ALL
CHASING OUR HEARTS' DESIRE
YET WE GO ON BELIEVING
NOTHING CAN HARM US

THIS IS FOREVER

(MUSIC swells as scene changes to Svetlana's hotel room.)

ACT II

Scene 5

A hotel room. SVETLANA and ANATOLY. As the scene begins they are singing their own version of YOU AND I.

SVETLANA.
YOU KNEW BETTER THAN ME
WHERE YOUR AMBITIONS WOULD TAKE US
I KNEW SOONER THAN YOU
THAT THOSE AMBITIONS WOULD BREAK US
YOU WOULD NOT BELIEVE ME
WHY SHOULD YOU BELIEVE ME?
I HELD YOU BACK
YOU AND YOUR DREAMS

WHO NEEDS A DREAM?
WHO NEEDS AMBITION?
WHO'D BE THE FOOL
IN MY POSITION?
YEAR AFTER YEAR
I'M STILL DENYING
ANYTHING'S CHANGED
ANYTHING'S DYING

BUT THEN—
SVETLANA & ANATOLY.
YOU AND I
WE'VE SEEN IT ALL

BEEN DOWN THIS ROAD BEFORE
  SVETLANA
BUT I GO ON PRETENDING
STORIES LIKE OURS
HAVE HAPPY ENDINGS.

(The song ends, they look at each other. Pause. ANATOLY turns away.)

ANATOLY. What is left to say?
SVETLANA. We've said everything. *(Beat.)* Over the years—we've said everything to each other. Haven't we?
ANATOLY. I never lied to you, Svetlana.
SVETLANA. Is she beautiful?

(Beat. He nods.)

SVETLANA. Is she rich?

(He smiles, shakes his head.)

SVETLANA. But she dresses well.
ANATOLY. Is that a question?
SVETLANA. No. *(Short pause.)* Are you happy? Is she?
ANATOLY. Svetlana, I love her.
SVETLANA. That wasn't what I asked. That wasn't what I wanted to know. *(Beat. She holds out her hand.)* Good to see you again. It is always a pleasure to see my husband.
ANATOLY. Svetlana.—

(She begins to cry. He holds her and comforts her. MOLOKOV enters with NIKOLAI. SVETLANA immediately goes out.)

MOLOKOV. It's been hard on her. (*ANATOLY says nothing.*) It's a pity how the innocent suffer. (*Beat.*) She of course has no apartment now. She stays with friends. She goes by trolley. There is no car either.

ANATOLY. She said nothing. But it doesn't surprise me; they would take everything of mine away. I'm not naive. (*Beat.*) I should go. It's late. Thank you for arranging this. Here. I doubt if she would take money from me.

MOLOKOV. Why don't you see. She will be around. She is staying for the rest of the match.

ANATOLY. (*Taken aback.*) I don't think that would be a good idea.

MOLOKOV. (*Suddenly yells at him.*) No one cares what you think anymore!!! (*ANATOLY is stunned.*) Not your wife. Not your brother.

ANATOLY. My brother?

MOLOKOV. There is a housing shortage in Rybinsk. He and his wife have had to find a smaller apartment.

ANATOLY. Because I left?

MOLOKOV. Did Svetlana tell you about *her* brother? Suddenly there is no room for him at the medical school.

ANATOLY. She didn't—

MOLOKOV. And then there's me! Someone had to be held accountable for your selfishness, Anatoly!

ANATOLY. Do not blame me!

MOLOKOV. You see how one little move, it affects many people's lives. Hurts so many people—

ANATOLY. I don't consider myself responsible for—

MOLOKOV. (*Pushing him in the chest.*) We do!!!

(*ANATOLY is very upset. Short pause.*)

MOLOKOV. Get out of my sight. Wait. (*Takes a piece of paper out of his pocket and hands it to ANATOLY.*) A statement made and signed by your colleagues at the Federation claiming the reason for your sudden departure was that a rather large sum of money had been found missing from their treasury.

ANATOLY. That's ridiculous, no one's going to believe—

MOLOKOV. There was an official hearing! No one spoke in your defense. At home, you are an embezzler!!

(ANATOLY is dazed.)

NIKOLAI. (*Quietly.*) Your brother's son is how old? Five, isn't it?

ANATOLY. Are you threatening—?

MOLOKOV. In what world do you live!!! What did you think you were doing, Anatoly?!!! (*Beat.*) Now get out. You disgust me!

(ANATOLY leaves.)

End of Scene

[MUSIC # 23: FREDDIE GOES METAL]

ACT II

Scene 6

Outside the Arena building. FREDDIE enters with REPORTERS and FANS, signing autographs.

FREDDIE. Five-three, ladies and gentlemen! That's two in a row! And I'm just hitting my stride!
(*Singing.*)
WHAT'D I SAY? TELL ME!
MAKE MY DAY—TELL ME
YOU GOT IT WRONG—HE'S WASHED UP
AND IT'S ME IN POLE POSITION
SPREAD THE NEWS—TELL THEM

IT'S A CRUISE—TELL THEM
I'M ON A ROLL
FLYING HIGH
WORKING ON HIS DEMOLITION

I KNOW THAT I'VE GOT HIM NOW
AND IT'S ALL DOWN TO THE DAY
WHEN I TOLD HER TO GET OUT OF MY LIFE
WHAT A MOVE!
WHAT'D I SAY?
THAT'S THE REAL STORY
YOU CAN REVEAL
ON MY OWN, IT'S BECOME
A WHOLE NEW BOARD GAME

I TELL YOU PEOPLE,
YOU'VE JUST SEEN A WHOLE NEW BOARD
GAME!

(*At the end, ATTENDANT is heard to say:*)

ATTENDANT. Miss Vassy, your car is coming.

(*FREDDIE stops. Silence. He turns and the CROWD
parts. There is FLORENCE.*)

FLORENCE. Congratulations. Nice game.
FREDDIE. Pretty dumb move he made.
FLORENCE. (*As a question.*) But we all make
foolish moves?
FREDDIE. Not me. Not me. (*He goes off to his
car.*)

(*REPORTERS disburse.
NIKOLAI comes up to FLORENCE, holding a coat.*)

NIKOLAI. I think this is Sergievsky's—
FLORENCE. Yes, I think it—

NIKOLAI. He left it at his wife's hotel room last night.

FLORENCE. (*Stunned.*) His—(*Beat.*) I'll give it to him. Thank you.

ANATOLY. (*Coming out—to Attendant.*) I need a fan in there! Or are they trying to torture me!!

FLORENCE. Here. Here's your coat, you must be freezing.

ANATOLY. I'm sweating. There's our car.

FLORENCE. Anatoly, I love you.

ANATOLY. This I know. I do.

(They exit.)

End of Scene

ACT II

Scene 7

[MUSIC #23A: CHESS UNDERSCORE]

Lobby of the Arena, as the match continues. WALTER stands, smoking. MOLOKOV comes out.

MOLOKOV. Not to let us smoke in there, it isn't civilized.

WALTER. Ivan! I heard you were here. I was going to look you up, but—You know how things get, never a minute to myself.

MOLOKOV. You've been promoted.

WALTER. Is that gossip? (*Laughs.*)

(Short pause.)

MOLOKOV. Not like Anatoly to seem so edgy. Perhaps it is the presence today of your Secretary of Sate that makes him nervous.

WALTER. Our Secretary of State makes no one nervous, Ivan. This is our problem.

MOLOKOV. I suppose there'll be photos with the players.

WALTER. Both of whom now live in America, choose to live in America! Sorry, Ivan. To you the world must seem very unfair.

MOLOKOV. (*Hands him an envelope.*) Here. Read this.

WALTER. (*Putting it in his pocket.*) I'll save it for—

MOLOKOV. Read. I want Anatoly back, Walter.

WALTER. (*Condescending.*) I know, Ivan. I know. And Florence? You going to shoot her with a poison dart?

[MUSIC #24: LET'S WORK TOGETHER]

MOLOKOV. (*Sings.*)
NOW YOU AND I WE'VE BEEN AROUND
WE'VE SEEN THEM ALL COME AND GO
WE DON'T NEED TO PUT EACH OTHER DOWN
WALTER.
THIS IS NOT WHAT I WANTED TO HEAR
TOO SINCERE
I DON'T WANT TO KNOW
MOLOKOV.
DON'T BE TOO QUICK TO CONDEMN
AND DON'T ASSUME YOU'RE ON TOP
WALTER.
C'MON IVAN YOU CAN'T WIN 'EM ALL.
MOLOKOV.
AND WHY NOT?
OR AT LEAST WE CAN GO FOR A DRAW.
WALTER. (*Has just taken a peek at the letter.*)
TELL ME MORE—

MOLOKOV.
ONLY TALKING SHOP!

(WALTER continues to read, as MOLOKOV sings.)

MOLOKOV.
THERE COMES A TIME WHEN WE SHOULD POOL
    RESOURCES
COULD BE THE ANSWER TO OUR NATIONS'
    PRAYERS
LET'S WORK TOGETHER FOR THE ONLY COURSE
    IS
TO MIX OUR LAISSEZ WITH OUR SAVOIR FAIRES
WE DO OUR BEST WORK WHEN WE HUNT IN
    PAIRS
    WALTER. *(Spoken.)* Bravo. Very nice. So her
father's alive.
    MOLOKOV. Yes, Florence's father is alive. He'd
been away.
    WALTER. "Away." *(Laughs.)* And of course he
won't be allowed to come to her. Not while she's with a
defector. *(Beat.)* I could try to prevent this, Ivan. Or do
you have a poison dart for me?
    MOLOKOV. If you're not interested in working
something out.
    WALTER. *(Sings.)*
I HOPE YOU DON'T MISUNDERSTAND
FOR I DON'T WANT TO CLOSE DOORS
WE'RE COMMUNICATORS AFTER ALL
    MOLOKOV.
WELL WE ALL HAVE OUR OWN POINT OF VIEW
MAYBE YOU
OUGHT TO STICK TO YOURS
    WALTER.
I LIKE TO BE MY OWN MAN
BUT IN THE LIGHT OF YOUR WORDS—
    MOLOKOV.
NO—THE LIGHT WAS IN THE ENVELOPE

WALTER.
VERY GOOD!
BUT IT'S TIME TO PUT RANCOR ASIDE
PETTY PRIDE
  MOLOKOV.
STRICTLY FOR THE BIRDS!
  WALTER.
THERE COMES A TIME WHEN WE SHOULD POOL
    RESOURCES
COULD BE THE ANSWER TO OUR NATIONS'
    PRAYERS
LET'S WORK TOGETHER FOR THE ONLY COURSE
    IS
TO MIX OUR LAISSEZ AND OUR SAVOIR FAIRES
YOU KNOW HOW MUCH THAT HELPS THE GUYS
    UPSTAIRS
  ARBITER. (*Over a speaker.*) Mr. Trumper has won
the nineteenth game. The score is now Mr. Sergievsky 5,
Mr. Trumper 5.
  *Monsieur Trumper a gagne le dix-neuviene jeu. Ils
sont maintenant a egalite cinq a cinq.*
  *Gah-spa-DEEN TRAHM-per VWEE-gral d'ye-vit-
NAHD-sit-ooh- you PAR-too-yoo. Ssh'yawt teh-P'YEIR
p'yat-p'yat.*
  *Herr Trumper hat dad neunzehnte spiel gewonnen. Das
ergebnis ist jatzt: Herr Sergievsky funf punkte, Herr
Trumper funf punkte.*
  MOLOKOV. Poor Anatoly. That's four losses in a
row. What he must be feeling ...
  WALTER. Hey, it's only a game!
  BOTH.
LET'S WORK TOGETHER AND THE WORLD IS
    SAFER
THE BERLIN WALL BECOMES A BACKYARD
    FENCE
AND OUR CO-OPERATION PAVES THE WAY FOR
OUR PRIME-TIME LEADERS AND THE MAIN
    EVENTS

BEHIND THE SCENES WE SHOW SOME COMMON
   SENSE
A LITTLE MUTUAL CONVENIENCE
LET'S WORK TOGETHER
   WALTER.
COMRADE!
   MOLOKOV.
BUDDY!
   BOTH.
IT'S OUR BEST DEFENSE.

[MUSIC # 24A: LET'S WORK—PLAYOFF]

ACT II

Scene 8

*An elegant restaurant. ANATOLY, FLORENCE and
WALTER finishing their dinner.*

WALTER. Sometimes you go through periods like
this. Don't worry, you'll get your form back tomorrow.
For every valley there's a hill.

(They eat. MAITRE D' enters.)

MAITRE D'. Excuse me, Mr. Sergievsky. There's a
telephone call for you.
   FLORENCE. Do you want me to—?
   ANATOLY. No. I'll take it. *(He gets up.)*
   MAITRE D'. This way. *(He goes. Pause.)*
   WALTER. You got the envelope? *(She takes the
envelope out of her purse.)* You'd said nothing, I
wondered—Is it at least possible that your father's alive?
Or are we talking about a hoax here?
   FLORENCE. Yes, it's possible! I think it's possible.

WALTER. I hesitated before—I didn't want to open a wound if—

FLORENCE. How can I see this man? I need to meet him.

WALTER. We'll have to wait to be contacted, Florence.

(MOLOKOV and SVETLANA enter; the MAITRE D' is ahead of them.)

MOLOKOV. Walter Anderson! The chess world is indeed a small world, isn't it!

WALTER. (*Shaking hands.*) Ivan.

MOLOKOV. And Ms. Vassy! We seem to have the same good food guide to Budapest. (*To WALTER.*) You've met Svetlana Sergievsky ...

WALTER. I haven't had the pleasure. How do you do?

(FLORENCE is taken aback.)

SVETLANA. How do you do?

MOLOKOV. And Florence Vassy?

SVETLANA. Hello. (*Beat.*) I've of course seen you at the Arena with Anatoly.

FLORENCE. I heard you were there.

MOLOKOV. (*To WALTER.*) How's the trout?

WALTER. Very nice, Ivan. Very fresh.

MOLOKOV. Then I shall not even open my menu. (*To SVETLANA.*) I think our table is ready. Excuse us, will you? (*They go to their table.*)

WALTER. If you want to leave ...

FLORENCE. Why would I want to leave? (*Short pause.*) She's quite attractive, isn't she?

WALTER. (*Trying to make a joke, puts his hand on Florence's hand:*) Anatoly has good taste. (*Laughs; FLORENCE doesn't.*)

ANATOLY. (*Enters.*) There was no phone call. (*Beat.*) When I went into the booth, a man came up to me and he told me that my brother's son had just today had an accident. Nothing serious. The boy was just very frightened. So were his parents. (*Beat.*) He thought I would be interested in knowing this.

FLORENCE. But how did he—?

MOLOKOV. (*Stands and calls.*) Anatoly!

WALTER. They just came in.

ANATOLY. (*To FLORENCE.*) He's with my—

FLORENCE. Your wife and I were introduced.

MOLOKOV. (*In Russian.*) Greeting from your brother. *Ti-BYEN pree-UYET ot BRAH-to.*

FLORENCE. What did he say? What did he say?

ANATOLY. He said my brother sends regards.

WALTER. (*Gets up.*) I'll go visit the dessert cart. Hungarian pastries are famous, aren't they? (*He goes.*)

ANATOLY. They want me back.

FLORENCE. What?!! (*Turns toward MOLOKOV and SVETLANA.*) Your wife?

ANATOLY. I don't know if I can take this.

FLORENCE. Take what?

ANATOLY. You've never been to Russia?

FLORENCE. You know I haven't. (*Beat.*) You want to go back. (*To herself.*) Christ!

ANATOLY. I did not say that.

FLORENCE. I know it can't have been easy—

ANATOLY. It's been very easy! (*Beat.*) With you, everything has been very good, Florence.

FLORENCE. Excuse me please. (*She gets up.*) I have to get some air.

ANATOLY. I'll come—

FLORENCE. No. I can be alone.

(*She starts to go to the terrace; SVETLANA suddenly stands and calls.*)

SVETLANA. Miss Vassy?

FLORENCE. Mrs. Sergievsky.
SVETLANA. When I met with Anatoly, he—
FLORENCE. Please. Would you excuse me? (*She turns to go.*)
SVETLANA. May I join you?
MOLOKOV. (*In Russian.*) What are you doing? *Shtaw tee D'YALE-a-ish?*
SVETLANA. May I join you?
FLORENCE. If you wish.
ANATOLY. Florence—
FLORENCE. I can take care of myself, Anatoly.

[MUSIC #25: I KNOW HIM SO WELL]

(They go out onto the terrace. Pause. They look out on Budapest.)

SVETLANA. Enjoying Budapest? Been here before?
FLORENCE. (*Smiles.*) A long time ago, yes.
SVETLANA. Things change though, don't they?
FREDDIE. Don't they.
SVETLANA. Treat him well. That is all I can ask, Florence.
FLORENCE. I've done my best. I've tried harder than I ever thought I could try. (*Starts to cry.*)
SVETLANA. I don't understand. He told me he loves you.
FLORENCE.
NOTHING IS SO GOOD IT LASTS ETERNALLY
PERFECT SITUATIONS MUST GO WRONG
BUT THIS HAS NEVER YET PREVENTED ME
WANTING FAR TOO MUCH FOR FAR TOO LONG

LOOKING BACK I COULD HAVE PLAYED THINGS DIFFERENTLY
LEARNED A LITTLE MORE BEFORE I FELL
BUT IT TOOK TIME TO UNDERSTAND THE MAN
NOW AT LEAST I KNOW I KNOW HIM WELL

FLORENCE.	SVETLANA.
WASN'T IT GOOD?	OH SO GOOD
WASN'T HE FINE?	OH SO FINE
ISN'T IT MADNESS	
HE CAN'T BE MINE?	HE CAN'T BE MINE?

BUT IN THE END HE
   NEEDS
A LITTLE BIT MORE
   THAN ME

MORE SECURITY	HE NEEDS HIS
I KNOW HIM SO WELL	FANTASY AND
	FREEDOM

SVETLANA.

NO ONE IN YOUR LIFE IS WITH YOU
   CONSTANTLY
NO ONE IS COMPLETELY ON YOUR SIDE
AND THOUGH I MOVE MY WORLD TO BE WITH
   HIM
STILL THE GAP BETWEEN US IS TOO WIDE

FLORENCE.	SVETLANA.
LOOKING BACK I	LOOKING BACK I
COULD	COULD HAVE PLAYED
HAVE PLAYED THINGS	THINGS DIFFERENTLY
SOME OTHER WAY	
I WAS JUST A LITTLE	WON A FEW
CARELESS—	MORE MOMENTS
	WHO CAN TELL
NOW AT LEAST	BUT I WAS
I KNOW HIM WELL	EVER SO MUCH
	YOUNGER THEN
	NOW AT LEAST

BOTH.
I KNOW I KNOW HIM WELL

SVETLANA.	FLORENCE.
WASN'T IT GOOD?	
WASN'T IT FINE	OH SO GOOD
ISN'T IT MADNESS	OH SO FINE

BOTH.
HE WON'T BE MINE?
DIDN'T I KNOW
HOW IT WOULD GO?
IF I KNEW FROM THE START
WHY AM I FALLING APART?

FLORENCE.	SVETLANA.
	WASN'T IT GOOD?
	WASN'T HE FINE?
ISN'T IT MADNESS	
HE WON'T BE MINE?	HE WON'T BE MINE?
BUT IN THE END HE NEEDS A LITTLE BIT MORE THAN ME	
MORE SECURITY	HE NEEDS HIS
I KNOW HIM SO WELL	FANTASY AND FREEDOM
	I TOOK TIME TO UNDERSTAND HIM
I KNOW HIM SO WELL	I KNOW HIM SO WELL

(As the song ends, NIKOLAI hurries out; ANATOLY hurries after him.)

NIKOLAI. *(In Russian.)* If you walk away like that again, you'll get it from me. *YEI-slee yee-SHOW ras tee tak ooh-ee-D'YAWSH, pah-LOO-chish ooh nain-YAH.*

ANATOLY. *(In Russian, to NIKOLAI.)* If you do, I'll ... *Tee SHTAW ska-ZAL, da ya tib-YAH ...*

NIKOLAI. *(In Russian, to ANATOLY.)* Fuck your mother. *H'YAWP tvai-OOH mat'l.*

(SVETLANA looks at FLORENCE , then at ANATOLY, and then goes with NIKOLAI.)

FLORENCE. What did he say?

ANATOLY. That the next time she walks away like that, he will strike her.

FLORENCE. Oh God.

(Short pause.)

ANATOLY. Florence—you mentioned nothing about your father.

FLORENCE. You know?

ANATOLY. Walter just—

FLORENCE. God damn him, he knew I didn't want you to—

ANATOLY. Don't you understand that they'll never let him leave while you're with me?

FLORENCE. Are you looking for an excuse?

ANATOLY. Now my defection is hurting even you!! What are they doing to us?!

FLORENCE. I don't know? What?! *(Short pause.)* Anatoly, let's go back to the hotel. The final game's tomorrow, or had you forgotten.

ANATOLY. I don't have to play. *(Beat.)* I'll tell the Arbiter that I need a week's postponement of the match.

FLORENCE. A week? You'll never get a week. The rules you agreed to—

ANATOLY. I need a week! I can't think. How the hell can I play chess if I can't think!!!

FLORENCE. Okay. I'll see what can be done. I'll go. *(Shouting after him as he goes.)* But it's not just the Arbiter who needs to agree!

End of Scene

[MUSIC #25A: GOING INTO
FREDDIE'S PITY ROOM]

ACT II

Scene 9

Freddie's suite. A FEMALE REPORTER, older than the earlier female reporter, sits with FREDDIE; three television TECHNICIANS set up lights, etc.

REPORTER. So you don't know *why* you started playing chess.

FREDDIE. Did Mozart know why he heard tunes in his head? (*He laughs as do the TECHNICIANS.*)

REPORTER. Then do you remember *when* you began to play?

FREDDIE. What does it matter? I'm playing now and that's what counts, right?

REPORTER. Of course.

FREDDIE. So then let's talk about now!

REPORTER. I was only hoping to begin with a little background ...

(FLORENCE is at the door. FREDDIE turns.)

FREDDIE. Look who's here. (*To TECHNICIAN.*) Watch out fella—she [Florence] might start humping your leg.

FLORENCE. Anatoly needs that break, Freddie.

FREDDIE. Anatoly who?

FLORENCE. Your opponent.

FREDDIE. Oh. How do you know him?

REPORTER. Maybe you'd like us to—

FREDDIE. No, there's nothing private going on here.

FLORENCE. Five days might be enough.

FREDDIE. Why should I? You know me, Florence, rules are rules.

FLORENCE. He needs to rest!!!

FREDDIE. You mean I broke him!! He's beaten, Florence, and you know it!!

FLORENCE. Maybe he is, but not for reasons that have anything to do with chess. (*Beat.*) As if you could ever understand such a thing?

FREDDIE. There's a lot more I understand now than when you—

FLORENCE. Right. Like Walter?

FREDDIE. He's a great agent.

FLORENCE. You're such a child. How can you be so gullible? (*Beat.*) A great agent, right. (*Beat.*) Forget it. You're gone, Freddie. And who knows, maybe you always were. Excuse me, I'm sorry to have bothered all of you. (*She goes.*)

FREDDIE. (*Calls after her:*) There are winners and there are losers and you are a loser, Florence!!! (*Short pause. He turns to the REPORTER.*) Where were we?

REPORTER. You were going to tell us about your background, Freddie.

FREDDIE. Yeah? (*Beat.*) Okay. (*He sits in front of camera.*)

[MUSIC # 26: PITY THE CHILD]

FREDDIE.
WHEN I WAS NINE I LEARNED SURVIVAL
TAUGHT MYSELF NOT TO CARE
I WAS MY SINGLE GOOD COMPANION
TAKING MY COMFORT THERE
UP IN MY ROOM I PLANNED MY CONQUESTS
ON MY OWN—NEVER ASKED FOR A HELPING HAND
NO ONE WOULD UNDERSTAND
I NEVER ASKED THE PAIR WHO FOUGHT BELOW
JUST IN CASE THEY SAID NO

PITY THE CHILD WHO HAS AMBITION
KNOWS WHAT HE WANTS TO DO

KNOWS THAT HE'LL NEVER FIT THE SYSTEM
OTHERS EXPECT HIM TO
PITY THE CHILD WHO KNEW HIS PARENTS
SAW THEIR FAULTS, SAW THEIR LOVE DIE
   BEFORE HIS EYES
PITY A CHILD THAT WISE
HE NEVER ASKED: "DID I CAUSE YOUR
   DISTRESS?"
JUST IN CASE THEY SAID YES

WHEN I WAS TWELVE MY FATHER MOVED OUT
LEFT WITH A WHIMPER—NOT WITH A SHOUT
I DIDN'T MISS HIM—HE MADE IT PERFECTLY
   CLEAR
I WAS A FOOL AND PROBABLY QUEER
FOOL THAT I WAS I THOUGHT THIS WOULD
   BRING
THOSE HE HAD LEFT, CLOSER TOGETHER
SHE MADE THE MOVE THE MOMENT HE
   CRAWLED AWAY
I WAS THE LAST THE WOMAN TOLD
SHE NEVER LET HER BED GET COLD
SOMEONE MOVED IN—I SHUT MY DOOR
SOMEONE TO TREAT HER JUST THE SAME WAY
   AS BEFORE

I TOOK THE ROAD OF LEAST RESISTANCE
I HAD MY GAME TO PLAY
I HAD THE SKILL, AND MORE—THE HUNGER
EASY TO GET AWAY
PITY THE CHILD WITH NO SUCH WEAPONS
NO DEFENSE, NO ESCAPE FROM THE TIES THAT
   BIND
ALWAYS A STEP BEHIND
I NEVER CALLED TO TELL HER ALL I'D DONE
I WAS ONLY HER SON!

PITY THE CHILD BUT NOT FOREVER

NOT IF HE STAYS THAT WAY
HE CAN GET ALL HE EVER WANTED
IF HE'S PREPARED TO PAY
PITY INSTEAD THE CARELESS MOTHER
WHAT SHE MISSED,
WHAT SHE LOST WHEN SHE LET ME GO
AND I WONDER DOES SHE KNOW
I WOULDN'T CALL—A CRAZY THING TO DO
JUST IN CASE SHE SAID WHO?

End of Scene

ACT II

Scene 10

The walk along the Danube. FLORENCE alone. A FIGURE appears in the shadows; it is NIKOLAI.

NIKOLAI. Miss Vassy?
FLORENCE. *(Turns, stunned.)* What?? What do you want with—?
NIKOLAI. We are able to see your father now.
FLORENCE. My father? Have you been following me?
NIKOLAI. Come with me, please. *(She doesn't move.)* If you ever wish to see your father.
FLORENCE. If it is my father. *(Beat.)* Why did you follow me here? Why didn't you come to the hotel?
NIKOLAI. I said we could see him. I did not say we had permission to see him. Hurry, please.

(They hurry off. BUDAPEST MUSIC as NIKOLAI takes FLORENCE on a "nightmarish" journey through Budapest which ends in a small room. NIKOLAI exits

and returns pushing an old man in a wheelchair. MOLOKOV approaches.)

FATHER. *(In Hungarian.)* It is you. *Ez te vagy.*

(FLORENCE turns to MOLOKOV.)

MOLOKOV. He recognizes you.
FATHER. *(In Hungarian.)* Her mother had those eyes. *Anyja szemeit orokoite.*
MOLOKOV. You have your mother's eyes.
FATHER. *(In Hungarian.)* My mouth, when I was your age. *Az enszam, a te korodban. (He laughs.)*
MOLOKOV. His mouth. When he was younger.

(Pause. She stares at the man.)

MOLOKOV. Do you—?
FLORENCE. I was four years old. *(She shrugs.)* I once saw a picture, but of a thirty-five-year-old man.
MOLOKOV. *(In Hungarian.)* She's seen pictures, but— *Feynke poket is tott, de—*
FLORENCE. Don't translate that, please.

(The father holds out a small photo.)

MOLOKOV. He has this picture. This was his proof. *(MOLOKOV hands the photo to FLORENCE.)*
FLORENCE. *(Trying to control her emotions.)* I'd never seen a picture of me as a baby before. *(Turns to Father.)* If you are my father, why didn't you try to find me?
MOLOKOV. *(In Hungarian.)* If you are her father, why didn't you try to find her? *Ha te vadj az apam miertnem kerestel engem?*
FATHER. *(In Hungarian.)* Ask the Russian. *Kerdezd meg az orosztol.*
MOLOKOV. Ask the Russian.

[MUSIC # 28: FATHER'S LULLABY]

FATHER. (*In Hungarian.*) Go, go, leave us alone. *Menyj! Haggyai minket egyedul.*
MOLOKOV. He wants to be alone with you. (*Short pause.*)
FLORENCE. Then go.

(*MOLOKOV leaves. The FATHER holds his hands out to her. She goes to him, to return the photo to him. He instead takes her hands. She sits down opposite him. He starts to sing:*)

[LULLABYE - *APUKAD EROS KEZEN*]

SLEEP MY LITTLE GIRL	*ALUDJ KICSI LANYKAM*
KEEP YOUR EYES CLOSED	*HUNYD BE SZEMECSKED*
ON THE WINGS OF SWEET DREAM	*ALMOD EDES SZARNYAN*
FLY UNDISTURBED	*SUHANJ KONNYEDEN*
ON YOUR DADDY'S STRONG HAND	*APUKAD EROS KEZEN*

(*FLORENCE recognizes the song; she starts to hum along, singing an occasional word.*)

YOUR PILLOW IS ASLEEP	*ELALUDT A PARRIAD*
SOON THE LAMP WILL SLEEP	*ELALSZIK A FENY*
FLY MY LITTLE GIRL	*SUHANJ KICSI LANYKAM*
ON THE BLUE SKY OF DREAM	*ALMOD KEK EGEN*

| ON YOU DADDY'S STRONG HAND | *APUKAD EROS KEZEN* |

FLORENCE. (*Closing her eyes.*) Father?

FATHER. (*In Hungarian.*) Father. *Apuked.*

FLORENCE. (*In Hungarian.*) Father. *Apuked.* (*In English.*) That means "Father," doesn't it? (*Beat.*) I remember that. (*She kneels at his feet; he continues singing, she hums.*)

YOUR LITTLE TOYS	*JATEKAID ARVAN*
ARE ASLEEP AROUND YOU	*VARNAK SZERTESZET*
SLEEP MY LITTLE ANGEL	*EGYETIEN BOGARKAM*

FATHER and FLORENCE

| SLEEP GENTLY LULLED | *ALUDJ KONNYEDEN* |
| BY YOUR DADDY'S STRONG HAND | *APUKAD EROS KEZEN* |

(*They embrace.*)

(*MUSIC swells as scene changes. SPECTATORS, REPORTERS, etc. are seen on their way to the chess match. Announcements are heard in English and Hungarian, welcoming all to the last day of the Chess Championship. As CROWD clears, ANATOLY is seen sitting alone in his dressing room.*)

ACT II

Scene 11

ANATOLY is alone in his dressing room, early morning; he has not slept all night. ENDGAME MUSIC begins. FLORENCE enters.

[MUSIC #29: ENDGAME]

FLORENCE. You slept last night in your dressing room?

ANATOLY. I didn't sleep. (*Beat.*) I either play or forfeit.

FLORENCE. I heard. You could appeal—

ANATOLY. To the Russian Chess Foundation? (*Short pause.*) Was it your father?

FLORENCE. You knew where I went?

ANATOLY. I was told. Was it him?

FLORENCE. Yes.

ANATOLY. I'm happy for you. Now you better leave me alone.

FLORENCE. Are you going to play?

ANATOLY. I don't know.

(*FLORENCE leaves. Singing of ENDGAME begins.*)

ARBITER'S ASSISTANTS.
DID YOU MAKE IT CLEAR THAT HE HAS TO BE
  HERE?
DOES HE UNDERSTAND
HE WILL LOSE HIS TITLE?
ARBITER.
HOW STRAIGHTFORWARD THE GAME
WHEN ALL ITS RULES ARE RESPECTED
ARBITER'S ASSISTANTS.
DID YOU MAKE IT CLEAR
THERE ARE NO EXCEPTIONS?
ARBITER.
...AND THESE RULES ARE THE SAME
FOR A CHAMPION OR FOR A NOVICE
NO SHOW, NO DICE, NO APPEAL, NO
  EXCEPTIONS, NO WAY!
MERCHANDISER'S ASSISTANTS.
DO YOU THINK HE KNOWS

WHAT IT'S COST HIM?
  MERCHANDISER.
DOES THE PLAYER EXIST
IN ANY HUMAN ENDEAVOR...
  MERCHANDISER'S ASSISTANTS.
DO YOU THINK HE CARES
WHAT IT'S GONNA COST HIM?
  MERCHANDISER.
... WHO'S BEEN KNOWN TO RESIST
SIRENS OF FAME AND POSSESSIONS?
THREATEN TO CUT OFF SUPPLIES AND HE'LL
  COME OUT TO PLAY
  RUSSIANS.
HE'S A BROKEN MAN
GOOD AS BACK IN MOSCOW.
  NIKOLAI.
IT'S THE WEAK WHO EXTOL
TAWDRY UNTRUTHS ABOUT FREEDOM...
  RUSSIANS.
WHAT A WAY TO LEARN
HOME IS WHERE THE HEART IS
  NIKOLAI.
...PROSTITUTING THE SOUL
CHASING A SPURIOUS STARLIGHT
TRINKETS IN AIRPORTS SUFFICIENT TO LEAD
  THEM ASTRAY
  C.I.A.
SELFISH LITTLE CREEP
EVERYBODY SUFFERS.
  BEN.
I'M NO EXPERT IN CHESS
BUT HAZARD THIS PROGNOSTICATION...
  C.I.A.
SELFISH LITTLE CREEP
EVERYBODY SUFFERS.
  BEN.
I'M NO EXPERT IN CHESS
BUT HAZARD THIS PROGNOSTICATION...

C.I.A.
SELFISH LITTLE CREEP
EVERYBODY SUFFERS.
  BEN.
THAT THE LATE MISTER "S"
HAS BETTER CHANCES OF WINNING
THE KENTUCKY DERBY THAN KEEPING HIS
  TITLE TODAY
  C.I.A.
SELFISH LITTLE CREEP
EVERYBODY SUFFERS
  C.I.A and BEN.
WE DON'T SEE THE JERK
EVEN COMING SECOND.
  JOURNALISTS.
WE ARE ALL AWARE
OF REPUTATION
BUT ONE EMPTY CHAIR
IS CONDEMNATION
OF A MAN WHO BLEW IT
SCUTTLED WITH DISHONOR
  MERCHANDISERS, CIA MEN.
NO ONE GIVES A DAMN
FOR HIS DILEMMA
JUST ANOTHER SCAM
WE'RE SICK OF THEM, A
LOT OF JOBS AT STAKE
WITH RUSSIA'S PRIMA DONNA
  ARBITER & ASSISTANTS.
WE CAN HARDLY BEGIN TO
IMAGINE WHY HE'D RISK ALL HE'S PUT INTO
HIS CALLING THROUGH THE YEARS
THE BLOOD, THE SWEAT, THE TEARS,
THE LATE, LATE NIGHTS, THE EARLY STARTS
  MORE JOURNALISTS.
OF COURSE THE EFFECT IS
EXACTLY WHAT OBSERVERS WILL EXPECT, VIZ.
THE WORLD IS SET TO CHEER

THE ONLY ONE WHO'S HERE
THE BAD GUY'S GONE AND WON THEIR HEARTS
  EVERYBODY.
IS HE STILL IN BED?
OR IN THE SHOWER?
EVEN IF HE'S DEAD
THEY WON'T ALLOW A
MAN TO SHOW UP AFTER THE APPOINTED HOUR

(*MUSIC builds to a climax. ANATOLY enters at last possible moment. As CROWD sees him, they whisper and point. PHOTOGRAPHERS take flash pictures. ANATOLY sits. Play begins. CHESS MUSIC.*)

  ANATOLY.
THEY ALL THINK THEY SEE A MAN
WHO DOESN'T KNOW
WHICH MOVE TO MAKE
WHICH WAY TO GO
WHOSE PRIVATE LIFE
CAUSED HIS DECLINE
WRECKED HIS GRAND DESIGN—
SOME ARE VICIOUS, SOME ARE FOOLS
AND OTHERS BLIND
TO SEE IN ME
ONE OF THEIR KIND
  (*Spoken.*) Pawn to G6. (*He moves.*)
  FREDDIE. (*Spoken.*) Concentrate.
  (*Sung.*)
SO HE'S GONNA FIGHT
THIS SITUATION.
WHERE'S MY APPETITE
FOR CONCENTRATION?
WHY IS HE SO FOCUSED
WHEN MY THOUGHTS ARE STRAYING.
  (*Spoken.*) Knight to E5.
  (*Sung.*)
LOOKING AT THIS MAN

IT'S HER I'M SEEING
ONCE MY GREATEST FAN
AND NOW HER BEING
HIS, STILL GETS TO ME
AND SCREWS THE WAY I'M PLAYING
    ANATOLY.
HERE I SEE A MAN CARING
ABOUT A MINOR SPORTING TRIUMPH, SHARING
A SHOW WITH ESOTERICS
PARANOIDS, HYSTERICS
WHO DON'T PAY ATTENTION TO
WHAT GOES ON AROUND THEM
THEY LEAVE THE ONES THEY TOUCH THE WAY
    THEY
FOUND THEM
IS THIS THE LIFE I NEED?
A CHILDISH, SELFISH GREED
    WHILE THOSE WHO LOVE ME BLEED TO
DEATH

THEN I THINK OF HER
HER AND HER FATHER
WHAT WOULD SHE PREFER?
I KNOW I'D RATHER
LIVE MY LIFE ALONE THAN FEEL
THAT I HAD HARMED THEM. (*He moves.*)

(*MUSIC.*)

    FREDDIE.
AT LAST HE'S MADE A MISTAKE!
    ANATOLY.
I CANNOT GO ON HURTING ALL THE PEOPLE
    WHO HAVE TRUSTED ME.
    FREDDIE.
HE WILL NOT ESCAPE FROM HERE!
    ANATOLY.
WELL HERE WE ARE—

THE FINAL STAGES OF A SOUL-DESTROYING
    GAME
THE SACRIFICE OF SOMEONE I WILL NEVER
    FIND AGAIN

FREDDIE.	**ANATOLY.**
CHECK!	NEVER!
CHECK!	NEVER!
CHECK!	NEVER!
CHECK!	NEVER!
CHECK!	NEVER!!!

FREDDIE. (*Sweeping towards victory.*)
BACKED THE LOSING SIDE
FLORENCE VASSY
TOOK YOU FOR A RIDE
FLORENCE VASSY
YOU JUST HAVEN'T GOT
THE INSTINCT OF A WINNER
    ANATOLY.
THERE IS NOTHING MORE TO DO
NO HOPE, NO WAY
TO SAVE THE GAME;
THE END OF PLAY!
SO I LOSE TODAY
AND TOMORROW.

(*ANATOLY turns his king down.*)

    ALL.
WE HAVE JUST WITNESSED HISTORY MADE
POWER MOVES WEST, ENDING AN ERA
THIS IS A GREAT DAY FOR AMERICAN CHESS!

(*WALTER rushes in followed by the CROWD, they go
    berserk. Chants of USA! USA!. FANS pull down the
    American flag and wrap FREDDIE in it as they carry
    him off. WALTER is last to exit.*)

End of Scene

{MUSIC # 29A: ENDGAME CONCLUSION]

ACT II

Scene 12

A room at the Budapest airport and later a hangar. SVETLANA and ANATOLY sit on their luggage.

SVETLANA. Why isn't the plane here?
ANATOLY. Why don't you go and ask someone?
SVETLANA. (*Hurt.*) Anatoly ...
ANATOLY. I'm sorry. Forgive me.

(He puts his arm around her and comforts her. The door opens and FLORENCE enters. She is taken aback, seeing ANATOLY hugging SVETLANA.)

FLORENCE. Molokov told me ... (*Beat.*) ... where to find you.

(Awkward pause.)

SVETLANA. Are you leaving too? Is that why you are at the airport?
ANATOLY. She and her father will soon be departing together.

(Short pause.)

SVETLANA. You must be happy. Where do you live in America?
FLORENCE. I've recently rented a small house in Connecticut.
ANATOLY. A lovely house.

SVETLANA. Your father, I hope, will be happy.

(A MAN enters.)

MAN. (*In Russian.*) You can board if you want: it won't be long. *Kha-TEET-ye, MAW-zhe-tyeh ee-TEE fsam-ol-YAWT. SKAW-ra pah-l' yet-TEEM.*
ANATOLY. (*To FLORENCE.*) We can board.

*(MAN has picked up their suitcases and leaves.
Pause.)*

SVETLANA. I think I shall go sit on the plane and wait.

[MUSIC #30: YOU & I—REPRISE]

ANATOLY. I'll join you in a minute.
SVETLANA. (*In Russian.*) Yes? *Da?* (*To FLORENCE, holding out her hand.*) Florence …

(They shake hands, she goes.)

FLORENCE. (*As soon as she leaves.*) You're doing this for my father—?
ANATOLY. No. (*Beat.*)
FLORENCE. If I ever thought—
ANATOLY. Will I ever see you again? (*Beat.*)
FLORENCE. No.
ANATOLY. I have an apartment in Moscow. I once again have an apartment in Moscow. (*Beat.*) If you ever … (*Beat.*) You could stay with us. It is a large apartment.
FLORENCE. Thank you. But I don't—

[YOU AND I]

KNOWING I WANT YOU
KNOWING I LOVE YOU

CANNOT COMPARE
WITH MY DESPAIR
KNOWING I'VE LOST YOU
   FLORENCE.
I'VE BEEN A FOOL TO ALLOW
DREAMS TO BECOME
GREAT EXPECTATIONS
   ANATOLY.
HOW COULD I LOVE YOU SO MUCH
YET MAKE NO MOVE?
   BOTH.
THERE WILL BE DAYS AND NIGHTS
WHEN I'LL WANT YOU MORE THAN I WANT TO
MORE THAN I SHOULD
OH, HOW I WANT YOU

YOU AND I
WE'VE SEEN IT ALL
CHASING OUR HEARTS' DESIRE
BUT WE GO ON PRETENDING
STORIES LIKE OURS
HAVE HAPPY ENDINGS
   ANATOLY.
YOU COULD NOT GIVE ME
MORE THAN YOU GAVE ME
I DON'T KNOW WHY
I'M STANDING BY
WATCHING THIS HAPPEN
   FLORENCE.
I WON'T LOOK BACK ANYMORE
AND IF I DO—JUST FOR A MOMENT
   ANATOLY.
I CAN'T IMAGINE A TIME WHEN I WON'T CARE
   BOTH.
BUT HERE WE ARE TODAY, AND IT'S OVER
HOLD ME AND TELL ME
WE'LL MEET AGAIN

FLORENCE.	ANATOLY.
IS IT OVER?	WHY IS IT OVER?

BOTH.
YOU AND I
WE'VE SEEN IT ALL
CHASING OUR HEARTS' DESIRE
BUT WE GO ON PRETENDING
STORIES LIKE OURS
HAVE HAPPY ENDINGS!

(As the song ends, he goes out the door; FLORENCE turns away. A FIGURE in silhouette appears at the door; MOLOKOV enters; FLORENCE turns.)

FLORENCE. Anatoly???

MOLOKOV. To see a man sacrifice himself, so a woman would find happiness ... Very touching.

FLORENCE. Is that what he's doing?

WALTER. (*Enters. To MOLOKOV.*) I was afraid you'd gone.

MOLOKOV. Would I do that? They're bringing him to the Aeroflot hangar. Now excuse me, my seat is being saved for me.

WALTER. Ivan.

MOLOKOV. (*Nods.*) Walter. Florence. You were such a beautiful couple. Reminded me of my wife and I thirty years ago. (*He goes.*)

WALTER. (*As soon as the door closes, WALTER laughs.*) You know, he's never even been married.

FLORENCE. (*Suddenly turns to him. Beat.*) No? (*Turns to where he left.*)

WALTER. (*After a pause.*) Florence, this is not easy to say— (*She turns back.*) The old man that Molokov— He wasn't your father after all. They were wrong. (*Beat.*) I'm sorry.

FLORENCE. Why are you saying this?

WALTER. Most likely your father died just like you thought.

FLORENCE. You're lying. (*Beat.*) Why are you lying?

WALTER. There was no proof. They said, nothing checked out.

FLORENCE. *I* checked out!!! I know it's him!!! (*Beat.*) ... there is the photograph—

WALTER. I guess, of just a baby. Some baby. Not of you.

FLORENCE. (*Yells.*) This is a picture of me as a baby with my father!! Look at it!!

WALTER. Florence, calm down. I can understand your being upset—

FLORENCE. (*To herself.*) Shit. Shit! How could I be so stupid?

WALTER. Florence, you hadn't seen your father—

FLORENCE. I mean about you!!! Why are you doing this? Why isn't my father here? (*Covers her ears.*) Who's going to be in that Aeroflot hangar?!

WALTER. They're releasing an imprisoned agent of ours. One of my people. (*Pause.*) Boy did they want Sergievsky back. Molokov's ego must have been very badly bruised.

FLORENCE. (*Looks up, shaking her head.*) You traded Anatoly for one of your agents?

WALTER. I took advantage of an opportunity. We suspected as soon as Molokov showed me the letter—

FLORENCE. (*Suddenly attacks him.*) You son of a bitch!!! I don't even know how to find my father. (*She turns away, dazed.*) No, please no. (*Short pause.*) Did Anatoly know all of this?

WALTER. Florence—

FLORENCE. (*Screams.*) Did he?!!!!!!

WALTER. It's my belief that he thought—

FLORENCE. What?!

WALTER. That you were getting your father back. And that's why he agreed. (*Beat.*) Finally agreed. They'd been after him since he got to Budapest.

FLORENCE. No!!!

(Short pause. WALTER starts to leave, then stops.)

WALTER. (*Suddenly turns to her.*) For Christ sake, I'm doing a goddamn job and I think I'm doing it well!!! (*Beat.*) The people of State told me they were happy with the outcome. I was taken aside and told this! (*Beat.*) What we've accomplished—Who knows, it could make a big difference at the summit. This is how things happen, Florence. We move, they move. Some trust gets built up. That's how it's played. (*He goes. Pause.*)
FLORENCE. Playing games!

[MUSIC #31: FINALE]

FLORENCE. (*Walks out.*) I was taken out of your arms. Then carried through an alley or under an archway. Everything was exploding around me. (*Beat.*) Just like it is today. (*Beat.*) The whole world seems to be exploding. If only we could start again, Papa. Be human again, Papa. If only we could. Anatoly! (*She sings the Anthem reprise.*)

HOW CAN I LIVE NOW?
WHERE DO I START?
LET MAN'S PETTY NATIONS TEAR THEMSELVES
    APART
MY LAND'S ONLY BORDERS LIE AROUND MY
    HEART

End of Play

APPENDIX

The following appendix is optional for the opening of Act II. It is "The Arbiter's Song," cut from the New York production. It can be found in the back of the Piano/Conductor's score and parts.

ACT II

PROLOGUE

Two months later, Kennedy Airport, New York. The First Class Lounge, Pan Am terminal. ARBITER stands surrounded by REPORTERS (mostly American) and his ASSISTANTS. There is luggage all around. Flight announcements are heard in the background. ARBITER'S SONG introductory MUSIC begins. The REPORTERS are shouting questions.

1ST REPORTER. How can you guarantee the safety of a guy who's defected?

2ND REPORTER. Mr. Stanos, won't the presence of the summit conference in Budapest tend to re-politicize—?

3 RD REPORTER. Without the Russian Chess Federation's support—

4TH REPORTER. One anti-Soviet speech by Sergievsky and the Hungarians—

5TH REPORTER. Do you really expect to keep control or are we now just riding this thing out?

6TH REPORTER. This time do you think you can control the player's actions?

(MUSIC stops.)

ARBITER. The first shit they give me, I say this to them!

[THE ARBITER'S SONG]

ARBITER.
I'VE A DUTY AS THE REFEREE
AS WE RESTART THE CLOCK
OF REMINDING ALL AND SUNDRY I TOOK
   GRAVE OFFENSE
AT EVENTS
IN BANGKOK

JUST A HINT OF TROUBLE THIS TIME AROUND
AND I'LL BE ON YOUR BACK
I WILL JUMP ON ALL OFFENDERS FROM A
   MASSIVE HEIGHT
DON'T INVITE
ANY FLAK

I'M ON THE CASE
CAN'T BE FOOLED
ANY OBJECTION
IS OVERRULED
YES I'M THE ARBITER AND I KNOW BEST
   CHORUS.
HE'S IMPARTIAL DON'T PUSH HIM HE'S
   UNIMPRESSED
   ARBITER.
YOU GOT YOUR TRICKS?
GOOD FOR YOU
BUT THERE'S NO GAMBIT
I DON'T SEE THROUGH
OH I'M THE ARBITER I KNOW THE SCORE
   CHORUS.
FROM SQUARE ONE I'LL BE WATCHING ALL
   SIXTY-FOUR

ARBITER.
IF YOU'RE THINKING OF THE KIND OF THING
THAT WE'VE SEEN IN THE PAST
CHANTING   GURUS,   WALKIE-TALKIES,
   WALKOUTS, HYPNOTISTS,
TEMPERS, FISTS
NOT SO FAST

I DON'T CARE IF YOU'RE A CHAMPION
NO ONE MESSES WITH ME
I AM RUTHLESS IN UPHOLDING WHAT I KNOW
   IS RIGHT
BLACK OR WHITE
AS YOU'LL SEE

I'M ON THE CASE
CAN'T BE FOOLED
ANY OBJECTION
IS OVERRULED
YES I'M THE ARBITER AND I KNOW BEST
   CHORUS.
HE'S   IMPARTIAL   DON'T   PUSH   HIM   HE'S
   UNIMPRESSED
   ARBITER.
YOU GOT YOUR TRICKS?
GOOD FOR YOU
BUT THERE'S NO GAMBIT
I DON'T SEE THROUGH
OH I'M THE ARBITER I KNOW THE SCORE
   CHORUS.
FROM SQUARE ONE I'LL BE WATCHING ALL
   SIXTY-FOUR
   ARBITER.
AS YOU SETTLE DOWN BEHIND YOUR PAWNS
POWER PASSES TO ME
YOU CAN PLAY LIKE FISCHER, CAPABLANCA,
   TAL COMBINED
I DON'T MIND

PLEASE FEEL FREE

THEY ALL THOUGHT THEY WERE THE BIG
   FROMAGE
BUT THEY DON'T HAVE MY CLOUT
I CONTROL THE MATCH, I START IT, I CAN CALL
   IT OFF
KASPAROV
FOUND THAT OUT

I'M ON THE CASE
CAN'T BE FOOLED
ANY OBJECTION
IS OVERRULED
YES I'M THE ARBITER AND I KNOW BEST
   CHORUS.
HE'S IMPARTIAL DON'T PUSH HIM HE'S
   UNIMPRESSED
   ARBITER.
YOU GOT YOUR TRICKS?
GOOD FOR YOU
BUT THERE'S NO GAMBIT
I DON'T SEE THROUGH
OH I'M THE ARBITER I KNOW THE SCORE
   CHORUS.
FROM SQUARE ONE I'LL BE WATCHING ALL
   SIXTY-FOUR
   ARBITER.
YES I'M THE ARBITER I KNOW THE SCORE
   CHORUS.
FROM SQUARE ONE I'LL BE WATCHING ALL
   SIXTY-FOUR

(An announcement is heard: "Pan Am Flight 803 to
   Budapest is now ready for boarding at Gate 12."
They start to go and the HUNGARIAN CHOIR begins to
   sing as the scene changes to Budapest.)

PROPERTY PLOT

<u>Prologue (Budapest, 1956 - 18 Partisans and Russians)</u>
Small wooden box to sit on
Small wooden box with chessboard (wooden)
2 bundles of books (18" high-valuable books)
Iron bedstead
Mattress for above on floor
Pillow
2 old broken bentwood chairs
Several suitcases (leather, beaten, period)
Small trunk (must be sat upon)
Several bundles of clothing
Clothing bags
Hungarian Peoples Republic flag (must be cloth) on a
    pole (8" to be cut down) with center insignia
    deliberately cut out
Several Hungarian newspapers (1956)
Several pipes, personal articles to be decided
7 rifles
6 automatics
2 pistols
Hang grenades attaches to some costumes
Ammo belts for partisans, etc.
<u>Scene 1 Hotel Press Conference</u>
Podium w/side shelves for water
5 mikes (not function) set on podium
Water pitcher on podium
Several glasses on podium
1 hand-held video camera
1 battery belt for above
Press cameras and strobes, functional
Tape recorders with mikes
Reporter pads/notebooks
Press identification for reporters
Checklist and pen for Hostess
Pens and pad

8 convention-type chairs (5 for reporters, 3 behind
    podium (Molokov, Anatoly, Freddie)
Tray with edible hors d'oeuvres
Small waiter-type towel
Tray with drinks (assorted drinks about 8)
Cocktail napkins on tray
Several drinks in hand (reporters)
Scene 2 Hotel Hallway/Anatoly Suite
Thai-style couch w/rattan cushion
Side table (modern, bamboo)
Telephone (on above table) will be rigged to ring
Upholstered, Thai rattan armchair
Side table
Chess set on above
Coffee table (Thai bamboo)
Several magazines (4-star hotel type)
Ash tray
Pile of phone messages
Attache case (Nikolai) (In case: file on Florence Vassy,
    binoculars, several papers)
Scene 3 Freddie's Suite
Several cans of Coke
Hilton Hotel towels (large, bath size)
2 large Thai-style armchairs
Low round Thai-style coffee table
Side table
Telephone on above
Several 4-star type Hotel magazines
Chess set
Plant in planter (brass planter)
1 large room service trolley w/untouched meal, a can of
    Diet Coke
Empty cigarette pack (Walter)
Briefcase w/ address book, pictures of feet, feet in
    sneakers, pamphlets (Walter)
Florence's shoulderbag w/notebook, pens, personal
    accessories as needed
Scene 4 - Merchandisers

Large display
Display items for above
Briefcases containing: paraphernalia and merchandising
    pamphlets
Business cards
Name tags with name and company logo
Attache case (Walter)
Attache case containing notes (Arbiter)
Name tags and Commemorative badges (Russians)
Name tags (Americans)
Name tags for Arbiter's assistants
Props for dancers (all in black/white checks):
    champagne glass
    push button umbrella
    teddy bear
    tennis racket
    hat
    ball
    vacuum cleaner
    bicycle
    baby carriage
    tablecloth
Scene 6 - Freddie's suite
Furniture repeats from I,3
Bangkok guide and map
Ash tray
Cigarettes (Walter) (he smokes this time)
Newspaper (American, Walter)
Food cart from I,3 still on stage but obviously finished
    with
Piece of paper with restaurant address on it (Florence)
Scene 7 - Streets of Bangkok
Bar
2 bar stools
1 bar table w/three chairs
Set of Maj Jong tiles
Money
Beggar's cup

Tray with drinks
Glasses on bar (6)
Towel for bartender

2 message tables
Several large white towels
Scene 8 - "Generous Sole Cafe"
1 large round table with lazy susan (48")
1 rectangular table for 4 (2'x4')
2 square tables (2'x2') for two
10 old, mismatched chairs (fake rattan)
Paper napkins
Silver
Chopsticks
Glasses
Soy sauce
Salt shaker (Anatoly's table only)
Chinese restaurant paraphernalia
1 short kitchen-type stool
Bangkok newspaper
White wine bottle
Full dinner (for man at table, main course is fish)
Menus
Tea cups
Tea
Full meal service for Molokov and Anatoly (Molokov eats
    his, Anatoly only picks at his)
Scene 9 - Arena/Florence's hotel room
Arena - same set up as Sc. 5

Florence's hotel room:
    Suitcases (she is packing)
    Rack (hotel type for suitcases)
    Clothes for packing
    Chair (nice, flat top)
Scene 10 - Underground garage
Headlight effect
Suitcase(s) Florence (same as I,9)

Letter (Walter hands to Florence)
Reporter gear (camera w/strobe)
Press pass (for reporter)
Wristwatch (reporter)
Scene 11 - Baggage Room/airport concourse
Boxes of freight
Watch (sound effect "beep")
2 luggage carts (kind you rent for $1 at airport)
Reporter's gear (from press conf., act I)
Hand-held cameras, lights, gear
Diet Coke
Small bag potato chips
Small bag airline peanuts
Several candy bars
Fresh pack cigarettes
2 oranges
ACT II - Scene 1- Budapest, (The Square outside the
  hotel)
Baby carriage
Peace banner
Step ladder
Scene 2 - Cathedral
Rack of votive candles
Taper for lighting candles
Scene 3 - Freddie's Suite
Settee
Armchair
Side chair
Low table
Rectangular table with phone
Railing unit
Pad/paper for Reporter
Coffee service
Room service menus
Scene 4 - River Bank
Park bench
Scene 5 - Svetlana's room - cheap State hotel
Single bed

Sheets
Blanket
Pillows
Wooden Headboard (Hungarian)
Arm chair (worn, old-padded back and seat)
Table
Desk with wooden chair
Wallet, money
Molokov's note (in Russian)
Side chair
Scene 6 - Outside Arena
Poster for chess match
4 autograph books
2 cameras
Scene 7 - Arena
4 stanchions and 3 ropes
Pedestal ash tray (tube type, buffed stainless, sand in top)
Envelope with letter (Molokov)
Scene 8 - Elegant Restaurant
4 tables, pedestal-type:
     1 seats 3 (Molokov, Svetlana,[Nikolai joins])
     1 seats 3 (Anatoly, Florence, Walter)
     1 seats 5
1 seats 2
Shaded candles for tables
Menus (15)
Silver, dishes, glasses, linen napkins, table clothes (for
     all tables)
Meals
Envelope (preset in Florence's purse)
Small tray for message
Message on tray (Waiter delivers to Walter)
Waitress trays (3)
Coffee served (2 tables)
Drinks served (2)
N.B. Molokov and Svetlana arrive too late for dinner—
     drinks or coffee only. Dinner is already on table for
     Anatoly, Florence, Walter. Dinner is in progress by

table for 5. Drinks only for 2 CIA men. Reserved sign
(in Hungarian—Molokov's table)
4 terrace chairs (stacked)
2 tables (stripped)
Scene 9 - Freddie's suite
Same as Scene 3 BUT:
> No coffee
> Add:
> 2 tv lights on stand (battery operated)
> Furniture re-arranged for interview
> Video camera
> Tape deck (shoulder style, headset for sound man,
> etc.)
Scene 10- Father's room
Wheelchair
Photo (man w/child)
Scene 11 - Endgame
13 chairs
Makeup kit
Magazine
Scene 11 - Arena
Flags - USA, USSR, GDR
Reporters, cameras
Chess table, set (repeat I, 5)
2 chairs
Scene 12 - Budapest airport
2 foot lockers
1 red cap cart w/luggage
2 anvil cases on wheels
Picture (Florence, repeat II, 10)

ONSTAGE TELEPHONES (Must be rigged to ring)

1) Anatoly's suite Bangkok
2) Freddie's suite Bangkok
3) Arbiter's chamber Bangkok
4) Freddie's suite Budapest

The following diagrams are of the New york setting, which consisted of twelve mobile periaktoid towers, six tall (numbers 1–6) and six short (numbers 7–12). Two sides of the towers were finished in a cast-cement look, and the third side consisted of six small periaktoi, which were changed by the operator inside the tower. During Act I, the finish was brass, except in Scene 4, when towers 7 to 12 changed to advertisements for the sponsors of the chess matches. During Act II, the finish was a gray wallpaper, in keeping with the old hotel in Budapest.

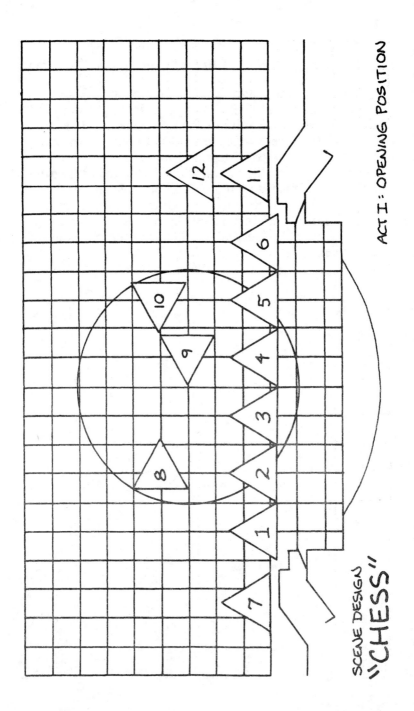

SCENE DESIGN
"CHESS"

ACT I: OPENING POSITION

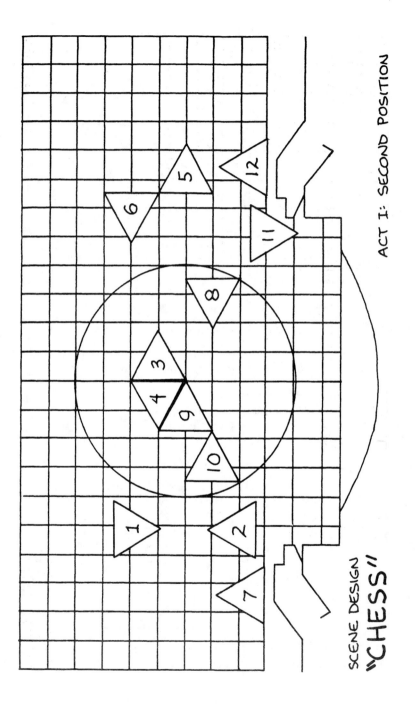

SCENE DESIGN
"CHESS"

ACT I: SECOND POSITION

OTHER TITLES AVAILABLE FROM SAMUEL FRENCH

THE MUSICAL OF MUSICALS (THE MUSICAL!)
Music by Eric Rockwell
Lyrics by Joanne Bogart
Book by Eric Rockwell and Joanne Bogart

2m, 2f / Musical / Unit Set

The Musical of Musicals (The Musical!) is a musical about musicals! In this hilarious satire of musical theatre, one story becomes five delightful musicals, each written in the distinctive style of a different master of the form, from Rodgers and Hammerstein to Stephen Sondheim. The basic plot: June is an ingenue who can't pay the rent and is threatened by her evil landlord. Will the handsome leading man come to the rescue? The variations are: a Rodgers & Hammerstein version, set in Kansas in August, complete with a dream ballet; a Sondheim version, featuring the landlord as a tortured artistic genius who slashes the throats of his tenants in revenge for not appreciating his work; a Jerry Herman version, as a splashy star vehicle; an Andrew Lloyd Webber version, a rock musical with themes borrowed from Puccini; and a Kander & Ebb version, set in a speakeasy in Chicago. This comic valentine to musical theatre was the longest running show in the York Theatre Company's 35-year history before moving to Off-Broadway.

"Witty! Refreshing! Juicily! Merciless!"
- Michael Feingold, *Village Voice*

"A GIFT FROM THE MUSICAL THEATRE GODS!"
– *TalkinBroadway.com*

"Real Wit, Real Charm! Two Smart Writers and Four Winning Performers! You get the picture, it's GREAT FUN!"
- *The New York Times*

"Funny, charming and refreshing!
It hits its targets with sophisticated affection!"
- *New York Magazine*